A LETHAL PAIR OF HANDS

Jessie saw the samurai's hands slip inside his tunic and she saw the flash of his *shuriken* star blade as it cut through the bonds around his wrists. His guard, who had been momentarily distracted by the bucking of one of the horses, had no chance at all as the samurai chopped the iron-hard edge of his hand down against the base of his captor's neck. The man dropped as if he had been shot.

Jessie stepped out from behind cover and levered a shell into her Winchester. "All of you, freeze!"

*   *   *

This title includes an exciting excerpt from *Sixkiller* by Giles Tippette. Follow the adventures of Justa Williams as he protects his family from the wild cutthroat Sam Sixkiller! Available now from Jove Books!

WESLEY ELLIS

LONE STAR

AND THE BLACK BANDANA GANG

JOVE BOOKS, NEW YORK

LONE STAR AND THE BLACK BANDANA GANG

A Jove Book / published by arrangement with
the author

PRINTING HISTORY
Jove edition / May 1992

ISBN: 0-515-10850-2

Jove Books are published by The Berkley Publishing Group,
200 Madison Avenue, New York, New York 10016.
The name "JOVE" and the "J" logo
are trademarks belonging to Jove Publications, Inc.

PRINTED IN THE UNITED STATES OF AMERICA

10 9 8 7 6 5 4 3 2 1

Chapter 1

Jessica Starbuck reclined on a leather sofa before a huge rock fireplace and listened to a West Texas storm buffet her sturdy ranch house. It was January and she knew that ten thousand head of her cattle would be drifting south with the wind. The temperature had barely risen above freezing this day and Jessie was concerned that it might snow or sleet before morning.

Across from her Ki appeared to be asleep, but Jessie knew that her best friend, protector, and samurai was very much awake. Ki was a man who could explode into action quicker than anyone Jessie had ever seen, but also possessed the gift of being able to achieve a complete state of relaxation. The samurai wasted no energy on the normal emotions of fear, anger, or revenge, but instead preferred physical action.

Jessie gazed around the huge Circle Star Ranch living room. Mounted on the walls were the heads of many trophy-sized game animals that her father had hunted all over the world. Jessie's favorite was the massive head and tipped horns of a Texas longhorn steer that had lived on the ranch for almost ten years and had led the spring trail drive north during every one of them. The steer had been as gentle as a dog and one of her father's favorites.

1

Everything Jessie saw reminded her of her late father, Alex Starbuck. It had been Alex who had built a multinational empire, quickly becoming one of the world's richest and most prominent entrepreneurs. Tragically, his money and power had attracted an evil cartel who had tried to recruit him into its design to capture and control the world's financial markets. When Alex had not only refused to join the cartel but had actually dared to oppose it, he had been assassinated on this very ranch.

Jessie studied an imposing picture of Alex Starbuck that rested over the huge stone fireplace. In the picture, which was a very good likeness, Jessie recognized not only the strength of her late father, but also his kindness. He had been good to her and, perhaps because she had been his only child, had taught her the things he would have taught a son. Things like how to run a ranch, ride a horse, shoot a gun or rifle, and how to be tough in business negotiations.

After Alex's death, Jessie had assumed control of the vast Starbuck empire and had quickly proven herself to be an excellent administrator. Quite often, she surprised and outwitted her managers and competitors alike because her remarkable beauty was such a contrast to her tough and decisive mind.

"Listen to this," Jessie said, picking up the newspaper on her lap and reading the headlines. "It says that a vicious gang in western Nevada has almost created a state of anarchy."

Ki opened his eyes. "Anarchy is a pretty strong word."

"Yes," Jessie said in agreement. "I'm sure that what we really have is some ruthless bunch that is going to come to a sudden and violent end when the authorities get organized."

"Why don't you read on," Ki suggested.

Jessie read a little more. "The newspaper is calling this the 'Black Bandana Gang' because they all wear black bandanas whenever they strike a bank, stagecoach, or even a train."

Jessie frowned. "Listen to this: 'The Black Bandana Gang is the most vicious seen in Nevada for many years. They think nothing of killing innocent men and women and, last month, even ran down a boy in the street while making their escape from a Carson City bank. Even more audacious, they have most recently murdered an esteemed territorial judge, Milton Archibald.' "

Jessie looked up quickly and with alarm. "Ki, he was one of my father's favorite friends! I knew the man very well. I have a lovely note and set of earrings that he sent me on my seventeenth birthday. Father and I spent a Christmas with him in Reno. He was wonderful. A committed bachelor with a great sense of dignity and warmth."

"And they killed him." Ki shook his head. "Does the article say that they did it out of revenge?"

Jessie finished reading the article, her eyebrows knitted with increasing concern. When she dropped the newspaper and looked up, her expression was grim.

Ki waited, hearing the storm batter the land and the sharp pop of the wood as it burned. The samurai understood Jessie very well and whenever he saw this expression on her face, he knew that she was both deeply angered and hurt.

"Ki," she said, her green eyes flashing, "the article went on to say that it is thought that Judge Archibald was murdered because of a possible gang member named Mose Pierce that he recently sentenced to hang. Mose was gunned down a few weeks later trying to escape."

The samurai stood up and stretched. He was slender and being half Caucasian and half Japanese, his skin was dark, his hair raven black. As was his preference, he was dressed in a loose-fitting black tunic and pants, and he wore a pair of sandals instead of boots. His long, lustrous hair was contained by a braided leather band.

"Is that everything?" he asked, reading her face and thinking that there was even more that was upsetting her.

"No," Jessie admitted. "It says that, when the judge was murdered in his house, there were probably two witnesses. Both of them have disappeared. One was a young man tuning the judge's fine old piano, and the other was a young woman who the authorities suspect was doing her weekly

3

ritual of cleaning house. Both have not been seen since the judge's murder."

"It would not give very good odds that they are still alive," Ki said.

"But why didn't the gang simply kill them on the spot?" Jessie asked. "That's the most obvious question and it isn't even addressed in this article."

Ki shrugged. "I don't know."

Jessie stood up and began to pace back and forth in front of her fireplace. She wore a man's heavy woolen shirt and although it was too big and she had to roll up the sleeves, it was plenty tight where it stretched over her ample bosom. Jessie's hips were slender, her legs long and tapered in her tight-fitting Levis.

She was, the samurai thought, a most graceful and beautiful woman whether in repose or in action. Her hair was strawberry blonde and the firelight made it shine like burnished copper.

Jessie stopped pacing. "I've got a business meeting in San Francisco in three weeks. Why don't we go early and see if we can get to the bottom of this business."

"You know I wouldn't mind," Ki said, "but the local Nevada authorities might have a different opinion."

Jessie waved off the objection with her hand. "I'm not saying I expect to help bring that gang to justice. I'm just saying that Judge Archibald was a family friend and that means that I would like to make sure that his murderers are brought to trial."

Jessie frowned. "Besides, there's nothing to do here in this foul weather that Ed Wright can't handle."

Ki nodded. Ed was the Circle Star Ranch foreman and an expert cattleman and rancher. "What about the storm outside?"

Jessie marched over to the window and glared at the dark, threatening skies. "I'll give it until tomorrow morning to clear," she announced. "And if it's still storming, then we'll see."

"See hell," Ki said with a tight grin. "You've already

4

made up your mind that we're leaving for Nevada even if this turns into a blizzard by tomorrow morning."

"Nonsense," Jessie said. "I'd wait at least until afternoon if that were the case."

Jessie returned to her leather sofa and resumed staring into the flames and, watching her, Ki was sure that she was remembering Judge Archibald and her father's untimely death as well. Both men had died violently and the parallel was quite obvious in that it involved good men who had been assassinated because of their high moral principles and courage.

"Jessie?"

She turned to look at him. "Yes?"

"We'll find out who killed the judge and why. I promise. If it's not done by the time you have to be in San Francisco, then I'll remain in Nevada and see it out to the end."

"Not without me you won't." Jessie managed a smile. "Meetings can always be rescheduled, Ki. But there are two young people—both guilty of nothing more than being in the judge's house when the assassins attacked—whose lives are either over, or in great danger. If we can also help them, then that will be icing on the cake for me."

"I understand. It's because of them that you don't want to wait any longer than necessary."

"That's right."

"If they are still alive," Ki said, "we'll rescue them."

"You know what really bothers me?" Jessie asked, turning away from the fire.

"What?"

"The newspaper didn't even give their names. It was like they were too unimportant to mention. Just a housekeeper and a piano tuner. That's all."

Ki said nothing but instead headed for his room in order to prepare for tomorrow's journey west. He knew that Jessie would also spend much of the rest of the day and evening preparing to depart. She would be up before dawn and, storm or no storm, out in the livery saddling her palomino, Sun, for the long journey.

5

Ki felt excitement about this adventure. Texas winters were harsh and he was sure that the sun would be shining in Nevada.

The Black Bandana Gang? Well, if he and Jessie had anything to say about it, they would soon be little more than history.

Jessie was up before dawn. The wind had died, but the air was very cold. She dressed as warmly as she could, pulling on her father's old cowhide jacket with its woolen lining over her shirt. Her boots were thick and well greased and she wore a pair of woolen long johns under her pants. Her Stetson, leather gloves, and a woolen scarf completed her attire.

Jessie headed for the ranch house kitchen where Mrs. Allen, their cook, had coffee, beef, and biscuits frying in the skillet.

"Excuse me for sayin' so," the woman remarked as she filled their plates, "but you are crazy to go out in that cold weather."

"Shoot," Jessie said, "there isn't even any snow on the ground."

"Too cold to snow."

Jessie shook her head. Mrs. Allen was a real worrier. Always had been.

"I got a feeling the storm is about over," Jessie said, sipping her coffee and digging into her breakfast. "By the time the sun is well up, it will be much warmer."

"And what about tonight? You're gonna freeze if you plan to make camp somewhere on the prairie."

"We'll find shelter," Jessie promised. "There's alway plenty of folks willing to take in travelers for a little cash."

"Phooey!"

"It's true. West Texas is dotted with little ranches. Most of them are struggling. They'll treat us like royalty for a few dollars. Don't worry, we'll be fine."

Mrs. Allen did not look convinced but since she knew

Jessie was determined to leave despite the bad weather, she busied herself in the kitchen, muttering, "I just don't see what's the all-fired hurry."

Jessie and Ki exchanged glances over their heaping breakfast plates. The food was hot and they both knew that they might not have a chance at a good meal until nightfall.

They ate their breakfast in silence and when they were full, Jessie wasted no time but grabbed her saddlebags and bedroll, then led Ki out the door.

As soon as they stepped into the cold, Jessie felt the bite of it on her face. It was well below freezing and there were no stars in the sky, which told her that the sky was still overcast.

Ed Wright had their horses ready. He was a tall, rawboned man in his early forties and since Alex Starbuck had died had become like a father to Jessie.

"This is just nonsense," Ed groused, as soon as Jessie stepped into the cavernous barn. "Jessie, what's the big hurry?"

She told him about Judge Archibald's assassination and the abduction of two young people who had been working for him.

"Well, freezing to death in a norther isn't going to make the good judge rest any easier in his grave."

"No," Jessie admitted, "but leaving now might help pick up the trail of what happened to that young man and woman who were abducted."

"Yeah," Ed reluctantly agreed as he tied Jessie's bedroll and saddlebags behind her saddle, "I can understand that."

Sun nickered and Jessie slipped the fine palomino gelding a dried apple. The gelding bobbed his head up and down with appreciation.

"Let's ride," Jessie said.

Ki nodded and when Ed pushed open the barn door, they rode out into the cold, predawn air.

"You headin' straight for Denver or are you going south through Santa Fe?" Ed shouted.

"We'll just see what the weather brings and then decide,"

Jessie told him. "Take good care of things around here while we're gone."

"You know I will."

Jessie smiled and reined her horse westward. Far behind her, the sun was just starting to worm its way over the eastern plains and she knew that it would not bring any appreciable warmth for at least a couple of hours.

She took a backward glance at her ranchhouse and then she touched spurs to Sun's sleek flanks. The palomino, well fed and cared for, lunged into a high lope. Ki's pinto was also a superbly conditioned animal and it fell into an easy, ground-matching stride.

Despite the intense cold that made her eyes tear and her nose run, Jessie felt wonderful. This, she thought as she swept westward across her frost-covered range, is adventure!

★

Chapter 2

For two bone-chilling days, they rode northwest across the vast Llano Estacado, or Staked Plains of northwestern Texas. Once, this had been the stronghold of the fierce Comanche and Kiowa. Only a few years earlier, in nearby Palo Duro Canyon, Colonel Mackenzie, operating out of old Fort Concho, had come upon an Indian camp in the deep canyon. A sharp battle had occurred and although most of the Indians had escaped Palo Duro, they had left behind their pony herd.

Colonel Mackenzie's theory was, that if you destroyed the Plains Indian's ponies, you rendered him almost harmless. That being his philosophy, Mackenzie ordered his soldiers to destroy the Indians' abandoned horse herd. Before the gunsmoke cleared that terrible day, over a thousand horses were slaughtered and the Indians were never again a threat in West Texas.

Whenever Jessie thought about that awful slaughter, it made her sick at heart. She loved horses and she was sure that the soldiers had felt awful about carrying out Mackenzie's orders. Closing her eyes, she could almost hear the sound of the cavalry soldiers' rifles as they grew hot and Palo Duro Canyon became clogged with smoke, dust, and the dying screams of a thousand Indian ponies.

That night, as with the two previous nights, they found a small ranch house where they could eat and sleep out of the elements.

"We don't have much," a thin, washed-out woman said apologetically. "But I can rustle up some biscuits, and just this afternoon we killed a chicken. Arnie has little whiskey but we've no coffee or sugar."

Jessie studied the woman's anxious face. She might have been twenty-five or she might have been forty. It was impossible to tell because the hard Texas wind and hot summer sun could parch a woman's skin and make it leathery in only a few years if she did not wear a bonnet.

"Ki and I have some dried apricots and prunes," Jessie said with an understanding smile as she studied the poor woman and her two teenage daughters. "Also some nuts and corn flour. Perhaps you could use them to make something nice."

The woman's tired face split into a wide grin and she looked at her daughters who were almost bouncing with excitement. "I think we could do that, don't you, girls?"

They were about twelve and fourteen, thin but healthy looking with corn-stalk colored hair and big splashy freckles. Their clothes were clean but patched over in patches and Jessie felt a pang of sadness because these poor darlings had probably never known the joy of a new dress or a good book.

Jessie went to her saddlebags and found the paper bags of nuts and dried fruit. She gave them to the children and watched them open the bags.

"Go ahead," she urged, "take a handful of each."

"No, no!" the mother said quickly. "That's for everyone tonight."

Jessie would not countermand the mother's orders. She wandered around the little dugout that this family called home and came to stand beside the samurai who was trying to look interested in the settler's homestead.

"I know this place sure don't look like much, and the soil ain't that good for farmin', but in good years, we raise

10

some pretty fine cotton and tobacco out here. I come from North Carolina, and there ain't no better cotton or tobacco country in the world 'cept right here in West Texas."

"I'm sure," Ki said, looking at Jessie for help.

Jessie said, "Mr. Bates, I'm sure that this is good country for cotton and tobacco, but I've seen the country down near the Gulf of Mexico and you might find it better farmland. The climate is a little warmer and they get more rain. The farmers down that way seem to do very well with about anything they put in the ground."

"Maybe they do and maybe they don't," Bates said defensively, "but this is our home and this is where we'll stay."

"I understand," Jessie said, realizing that this man would rather see his family live in poverty than admit that he had chosen to homestead land that would never give them more than a bare subsistence. It was a case of stubborn pride and Jessie had little tolerance for it when it affected women and children.

"I'm glad you understand," the farmer said, kicking his toe at the hard, flinty ground. "If we could just get a little more rain up in this part of the country, this'd be a paradise. I own nearly a thousand acres hereabouts."

"Is that right?" Jessie tried to look impressed but it was a struggle. On the Llano Estacado, a thousand acres would support less than a hundred cows in the drier years.

"It's a fact, miss. Now I can tell by the fancy horses you and your man here are riding that a thousand acres might not be big shakes to you, but in these parts, it makes me one of the major landholders."

"My, my," Jessie said, wanting nothing more than to turn this man's voice off and go inside to eat, then sleep.

"I mean to buy me some cattle," Bates was saying. "The trouble is, cattle wander and whenever this country is hit by a blizzard, cattle will walk until they either drop, run into a gully and die, or else just disappear. And I ain't no good with a rope or ridin' horses."

"You'd better stick with corn, cotton, and tobacco," Jessie said.

11

"Well, I dunno," Bates said, shaking his head because he was the kind of man too prideful to take good advice, "I'll just have to see."

"I'm cold," Jessie said, "why don't we go inside and sit beside the fire?"

Ki nodded eagerly, more because he was also growing impatient with this man's foolishness than because of the cold.

"You folks go ahead on in and warm up," Bates said. "I've got to check to make sure that all our chickens are still in the barn. Been keepin' them there all during this cold weather, but last week we ran out of corn and so I had to let them scratch around outside. Come sundown, sometimes they wander a little far. Coyotes get 'em if the children aren't watchin' 'em every damn minute."

"I understand," Jessie said, appalled at the thought that this man would have his daughters standing around in this numbing cold standing guard over a flock of chickens.

The dugout was humble, to say the least. Yet Mrs. Ida Bates had somehow managed to make it comfortable. There was a rock fireplace and chimney with a pipe that poked up through the prairie. The walls dug inside the hillside were packed and brushed and there were even a few pictures hanging from them. Two Indian horse blankets covered the floor and Bates had constructed beds, a table, and four chairs from what appeared to be salvage timber off a wagon. There was even a glass window set into the sod wall that fronted the dugout and the door was wood, rather than of hide that was typical of the humblest frontier dugouts.

When Jessie pushed inside out of the cold, the warmth of the dugout felt good and the smiling, excited faces of the girls greatly improved her disposition.

"I'm glad you decided to come inside," Ida told her. "I know that when Mr. Bates gets to talking about this place, he gets so excited and filled with big plans that, sometimes, he just rattles on and on."

"It's important for a man to be excited about his livelihood," Jessie said.

"I know," the woman replied a little wistfully, "but I just wish that excitement would help us make a better living here. Poor Mr. Bates gets so discouraged sometimes."

"Maybe things will be better this next year. If they're not, I suggested to your husband that he might consider moving you and the children down around Brownsville by the coast."

But Ida shook her head. "He's afraid that Mexico is going to march north again. He thinks they're fixin to try and win back Texas. Miss Starbuck, the main reason my husband won't move south is because of the Mexican army."

Jessie could do nothing but shake her head. Mexico's army was in disarray and General Santa Anna no longer had any influence or authority. The idea of Mexico marching north was about as realistic as thinking the Plains Indians would again rise up to take back their traditional hunting grounds.

"Well," she said, looking at the children, "I have a ranch about a hundred miles southeast of here. It's called the Circle Star. If anything ever happens to you or Mr. Bates and you need some help, you come find me."

"You mean that truly?"

"I do," Jessie said. "Those children need friends and schooling. I don't think that either you or those lovely daughters should need . . ."

The door opened suddenly and Mr. Bates, a scowl on his face, said, "What don't you think my missus or my daughters need, Miss Starbuck?"

Jessie was exasperated enough with the selfish, prideful fool to have told him right then and there that, because of his stubbornness he was needlessly causing his family to suffer. But before she could reply, Ida Bates was pushing between them, a smile frozen on her weary face.

"It's nothing," she said, helping her husband out of his coat. "Nothin' at all. Now you just wash up and get ready for a special dinner."

Bates gave Jessie a hard look. It was obvious that he didn't believe his wife and he'd probably harangue her later for her deception, but there was nothing Jessie could do about that now. She had seen too many frontier women like Mrs. Ida Bates. They were beaten down by dominating men, dominating land, and too much sky, silence, and empty space.

That evening they ate very well and Jessie entertained everyone except Mr. Bates with stories of the many peoples and cultures she had come to know during her travels as head of the Starbuck Enterprises.

"My, my," Mrs. Bates said almost dreamily. "I can't imagine why someone like you would bother to travel an ugly country like this in the wintertime."

"Ida!" her husband snapped.

The woman realized her error at once and made a pathetic attempt to repair the damage. "I just meant that this is a hard country in the summer and winter. Now in the springtime, when the flowers are like a quilted blanket across . . ."

"Why don't you just shut up!" Bates demanded.

The words died on Ida's lips. She looked away quickly and Jessie was immediately torn between wanting to comfort her and choke her overbearing husband.

"Let me see," Jessie said, "how about a bedtime story for the children?"

The girls, whose names were Minnie and Mary, beamed and Jessie managed to avoid an unpleasant confrontation with their father by telling a long, long fairy tale.

That night it snowed, but their horses were in the old barn and it was reasonably warm in the dugout. In the morning, the sky was clear and the sun was shining.

"Looks like a beautiful day for traveling," Bates said, unable to hide his eagerness that they leave.

Jessie hugged the girls and Ida, promising to stop by if possible on their return.

"Mr. Bates," she said just before mounting her horse. "I know that you are a very generous man and would never ask for recompense for putting us up for the night, but please take this for your trouble and expense."

She handed the man twenty dollars and saw his jaw drop.

14

"Why, miss, I . . . well, I sure do thank you!"

"And we thank you," Jessie said, looking right at Ida Bates.

Jessie mounted her horse, waved at the poor woman and her children, then touched spurs and galloped away with the samurai at her side.

"That man's eyes sure popped when you paid him. He would have been happy with one or two dollars."

"I know," Jessie said with a smile.

They rode along in silence for almost another hour, enjoying the newfound warmth of the winter sun and the sparkling ocean of melting snow.

"Say, Jessie?"

She pulled her horse up. "Yeah?"

"How much money did you leave her?"

"Who?"

Ki chuckled. "You know who."

"A hundred dollars," Jessie said. "That poor woman or one of her daughters will discover it in the only decent cooking pot she owns."

The samurai's lips split into a wide grin. "I left a twenty dollar gold piece in their empty coffee tin."

Jessie glanced sideways at the samurai and then they both began to laugh.

★

Chapter 3

Their ride to Denver was largely uneventful and Jessie, as always, was surprised by the growth of this high-plains town nestled at the eastern base of the towering Rocky Mountains.

"I think this town is going to eclipse Santa Fe," she told Ki as they rode down busy Larimer Street and came to a stop before Wardlow's Livery.

Jessie dismounted, then began to untie her saddlebags as the livery owner came out to greet them.

"Well if it ain't one of my favorite little ladies, Miss Jessica Starbuck!" Ed Wardlow bellowed loud enough to be heard in Golden. "What a surprise!"

Jessie allowed the big, smelly man to give her an affectionate bear hug. She liked Ed very much, it was just that he was a little overexuberant at times and she always worried that he was going to injure her back.

"How are you, Ben?"

"Never been better but had less," he said with a wink.

He always said the same thing. Jessie knew that Wardlow was a very successful man. "We're getting on the train tomorrow for Reno then Sacramento. I've business in San Francisco that will take a couple of weeks."

"You just leave your horses in my care and they'll love

16

you forever!" Wardlow boomed.

"I know that," Jessie said, feeling very assured that Sun and Ki's flashy pinto would have the best of everything while boarded in Denver.

"Won't you come by the house for supper?" Ben asked. "My wife sure would be pleased to bake you a pie and you know what a good cook she is."

"I sure do," Jessie said, "but we're tired and the train leaves early tomorrow morning, unless they've changed their schedule since the last time I was passing through."

"Nope, still leaves at 7 A.M. sharp."

"Then how about we have dinner when we come back through?"

"That'll be our pleasure," Ben said. "But the missus will still want to bake you a pie and leave it at whichever hotel you're staying at tonight."

"The Fremont."

"Yeah," Ben said, winking, "nothing but the best, huh, Miss Starbuck?"

"That's why I chose your stable."

It was the truth and very flattering. Ben Wardlow loved it, and before he and Ki led the horses inside where they would be curried to a shine, then fed, Jessie said, "Ki, I'll go along and get us rooms at the Fremont."

Ki nodded. "I'll be along in a minute or two. Sure you don't want to wait?"

"No," Jessie said, "just come along soon."

"Save some hot water for me."

"I'll order a tub for each of our rooms," Jessie said, heading up the wide boardwalk.

The Fremont was only half a block from the livery but Denver was such a bustling town that Jessie had to thread her way through a busy throng of rough miners, cowboys, and freighters.

"Hey!" a big, bearded miner shouted to his friends as Jessie walked past. "Would you just take at look at that pretty little swinging ass!"

The miner and his friends hooted with appreciation at

17

Jessie's neatly rounded buttocks and the outline of her long legs.

Jessie frowned but kept walking. She was hungry, dirty, and tired. Tomorrow, she and Ki would board the Denver Pacific Railroad Line that ran one hundred seven miles north to connect them with the Union Pacific Railroad in Cheyenne, Wyoming. From Cheyenne, they would ride a first-class coach all the way to Reno, Nevada in luxury and comfort. The worst part of the journey, Jessie knew, was behind them.

"Hey, honey!" the miner said, coming up behind her and breathing whiskey fumes on Jessie's neck. "How about you and me finding a pile of hay or something where we could have some fun."

Jessie stopped dead in her tracks and the big miner knocked into her. She turned around, doubled her fist and punched the man right in the nose.

"Ouch!" he cried, grabbing his face and then seeing blood on his hand. "Why you might have broke it!"

Jessie glared at him and his friends. "You're drunk and obnoxious. Go sober up and behave."

The man blinked. "Well goddamn you! You had no right to hit me thataway!"

"Where I come from down in Texas," Jessie said, "better men than you would be hanged from a cottonwood tree for accosting a lady."

"A—what!"

"For bothering a lady!"

"You ain't no lady," another miner sneered. "Ladies don't wear men's pants, shirt, and coat. And they don't pack sixguns on their hips, neither! You look like a little hussy to me."

Jessie started to grab the gun on her hip but a miner anticipated this and his hand clamped down on her forearm. "Now, now. Don't be makin' another big mistake. Maybe all we want is a kiss."

"I'll give you a kiss," Jessie snarled.

"You will?"

"In hell!" she cried as she drove her knee up into the man's crotch.

"Ahhh!" he yelped, grabbing his testicles and folding to his knees.

"Well sonofabitch!" the first miner with the bloody nose cried. "Now you really got us mad!"

Jessie kicked another one in the shins and managed to get in a second hard punch before she was overpowered and lifted off her feet.

"Ki!" she cried. "Ki, help!"

Less than a hundred yards away, Ki heard Jessie's cry and bolted from the livery. Since the boardwalk was packed, he sprinted down the center of Larimer, dodging freight wagons and horsemen alike.

He just had a glimpse of the miners dragging Jessie into an alley between a dress shop and a saloon, but that was all that he needed.

Ki reached inside his tunic and yanked out one of his favorite and most devastating samurai weapons. It was called a *han-kei*, which was a half-sized version of the traditional *nunchaku*. The *nunchaku* was a popular fighting weapon because of its simplicity and effectiveness against many enemies in close-quarter combat. Comprised of two seven-inch long sticks that were attached by a piece of braided horsehair, the *han-kei* that Ki preferred was a fearful weapon when he gripped one stick and whirled the second.

The sticks were made of hardwood and smoothed on one side so that they fit perfectly together. Now, as Ki plunged into the alley and found the miners attacking Jessie, he screamed and the *han-kei* smashed into a man's skull, crushing it.

The miners whirled to face him. Several went for their pistols and felt the terrible force of the *han-kei* as bones were shattered in hands, arms, and faces.

"Get him!" yelled the miner with the bloody nose.

But men were falling back as the samurai's whirling weapon cut them down like wheat before the sickle. The big miner who had already ripped Jessie's shirt open snarled and grabbed his knife. He lunged in so close that Ki had to retreat a step and now, he grabbed both sides of the *han-kei* and thrust them at the miner's face.

"Ahhhh!" the man wailed in agony, as one of the sticks gouged his eye to jelly.

Ki stepped back and those miners still able to stand scattered and ran for their lives.

"He blinded me!" the miner shrieked.

"I ought to have killed you," Ki hissed as he reached out and helped Jessie to her feet. Looking at her pale face, he turned and raised his hand, fingers outstretched and stiff.

"No!" Jessie lowered her voice. "Let him live. He will remember this hard lesson every day of his life."

Ki dropped his hand. With its rock-hard edge, he could have smashed the base of the man's neck and broken it as easily as he might have a twig.

"I'm all right," Jessie promised.

The samurai looked at the fallen miners, one of them dead, several of them seriously injured by his *han-kei*.

"You should never touch or even speak to a lady," he advised his victims.

"Who in God's name are you!" a miner cradling a broken wrist sobbed.

"I am samurai and *ninja*."

"You're worse than a nightmare!"

Ki took a menacing step toward the man who sobbed and covered his head. "No, please. Don't kill me, mister!"

"Ki!"

The samurai relaxed. He folded up his *han-kei* and slipped it back inside his black tunic. He gave Jessie his arm after she covered herself by rebuttoning her torn shirt.

"With too many people come bad things," Ki said philosophically.

"Yes," Jessie said, turning her back on the carnage of humanity that lay like garbage around them. "Come on, let's get those rooms and a bath. They made me feel even dirtier."

Ki understood. He wondered if these men would bring friends and want to kill him for killing one of their kind and hurting so many more.

It didn't matter. If they came out of vengeance, they would die in vengeance.

Chapter 4

That evening after cleaning up but before dinner Jessie and Ki went to the sheriff's office and made a full report. Sheriff Jim Weaver was not pleased.

"These miners can be pretty crazy when one of their own is killed or hurt. I can't promise you that there won't be some retribution."

"But they tried to rape me in the alley!" Jessie protested in anger. "What kind of law is there in Denver?"

"Now just a damn minute!" Weaver snapped. "Me and my deputies do the best that we can, considering that we're two positions short."

"Well, Sheriff, all I know is that those miners would have attacked any unescorted woman that had been forced to pass among them."

"They'd probably been drinking too much," the sheriff argued. "But that don't mean that one of them should have been killed or half blinded by your Chinese henchman."

Jessie's temper flared. "He's not a 'Chinese henchman' and if he hadn't have come to my rescue, *I* might have been killed."

The sheriff scowled. "I've already talked to a few of them and they say they were just having a little fun."

"Fun!"

"Okay, so the fun got out of hand," the sheriff groused. "Still, no one should have been killed."

"How about some protection until our train leaves in the morning?"

"Sounds to me like you already got all the protection you need," the sheriff said testily. "Best thing you can do is stay off the streets and leave town as quietly as possible."

"Thanks a lot," Jessie said with more than a hint of contempt. "Ki, let's get out of here."

They left and went directly to the Fremont Hotel. Both Jessie and Ki had baths and changed into clean dinner clothes and went downstairs to the lobby.

"Excuse me," a well-dressed man in a starched collar and frock coat called from across the room. "May I have a word with you, please?"

Jessie frowned. She was starving and in no mood to chat with a stranger. This man was middle-aged with muttonchop whiskers and a slightly disheveled appearance.

"I'm with the *Rocky Mountain News*," he announced, producing a pad and pencil. "And I understand that you are Miss Jessica Starbuck of Texas."

"I am," Jessie sighed, "but I really don't have . . ."

"And this," the reporter interrupted, "is Ki! The man who killed one of our miners with a flying stick?"

"It's called a *nunchaku*," the samurai corrected, "and I was simply protecting Miss Starbuck from a vicious attack."

The newspaperman raised his eyebrows. "I hear there are several sides to that story. Apparently, you are free on bail?"

"Bail?" Jessie said. "There were dozens of witnesses. Talk to them if you want a story. Ki has been charged with nothing. In fact, he ought to receive a mayor's commendation for his actions. What happened to me could have happened to one of your own respectable lady citizens."

"Perhaps," the newspaperman said, "but I understand that you were not exactly dressed as a lady when the attack took place. Rather, they say that you were dressed in a man's clothing."

23

"That's true. Ki and I have been riding hard from Texas. You don't cross eight hundred miles of wilderness dressed in a frilly riding habit and riding a sidesaddle."

The man looked embarrassed. "Yes, that's true, but you must admit, that wearing . . ."

Jessie had heard enough. "Excuse us," she said, "but we have a table reserved."

"But I have a number of questions! Would you mind if I joined you?"

"Yes I would," Jessie said, brushing past the man.

"Not very friendly, is she," the reporter complained.

Ki almost dropped the man but decided instead to let the remark pass before he followed Jessie into the hotel restaurant to dine.

They ordered speckled trout and all the trimmings along with a green salad and apple pie for desert. Jessie ate every morsel and so did the samurai and when their hunger still wasn't satisfied, they shamelessly ordered another helping of pie, this time cherry.

"Ahh," Jessie said when they were finally done with their meal, "I feel better now. I'd feel even better yet if that newspaper reporter wasn't waiting out in the lobby to accost us the minute we leave our table."

"I can take care of him."

"No," Jessie said, "let's just try to ignore the man and go upstairs to our rooms and retire for the night."

When the check was paid and they stood up to leave, Jessie said, "Uh-oh."

The samurai pivoted around to see that three huge miners were standing out in the lobby and he saw the newspaper reporter pointing into the dining room.

"I don't want trouble in here," Jessie whispered, looking around the room at the other diners, many of whom were older and possessing delicate constitutions.

"I doubt we have much of a choice," Ki said as the three miners came marching across the dining room in their direction.

The samurai stood up and moved a half step from their

24

table. Jessie reached into her purse and found the lethal two-shot derringer her father had given her when she was still a girl. She cocked the derringer and left her hand in her purse.

"You're coming with us," the largest of the three miners growled. "Now."

"I don't think so," Ki said. "I have other plans for the remainder of the evening."

"Change 'em."

Ki shook his head and when the miner reached for his gun, the samurai delivered a "knife-hand strike" just as the miner's gun was clearing leather. Everyone in the room heard the man's wrist-bones snap an instant before he cried out in pain and the gun clattered on the polished hard-wood floor.

The other two miners recoiled, both foolishly going for their guns, but when Jessie thrust her ominous-looking little derringer at them and cocked the hammer, they froze.

"Take your friend," Jessie ordered, "and get out of this hotel while you are still able."

The one with the broken wrist was moaning and cursing as his two companions quickly led him away. But at the door one of them turned and shouted, "You ain't seen the last of us! You just wait and see!"

Jessie uncocked her derringer and returned it to her purse before she slipped her arm through Ki's and they moved to the door with everyone in the room gaping at them.

"Please!" the reporter said, falling in beside them as they moved toward the stairs leading up to their rooms. "All I'm asking for is a story."

Jessie's green eyes glittered. "There is no story. We were confronted, then as now, and we defended ourselves. That's it."

"Then you," the reporter said, turning to Ki. "You're the one that really interests me. What kind of strange fighting style enables you to render much bigger men than yourself so helpless?"

"It is called '*te*,'" the samurai replied, "and that means 'empty and fighting.'"

25

"I never heard of it." The reporter jumped in front of them and blocked their exit up the stairs. "Is it some. . . ."

Ki raised his hand but Jessie took mercy on this poor fool. "Go ahead, Ki, tell the man. He's probably been assigned by his editor to either come back with a story, or come back dead on his shield."

The samurai had about run out of patience with this man, but he patiently explained. "*Te* is the art of fighting in which one's body becomes the ultimate weapon. It was developed by the Okinawans after they were conquered by the Japanese and suffered the indignity of not being allowed traditional weapons."

The reporter was scribbling furiously. "So you mean it is some kind of weird way of hitting with your fist."

"Not the fist," Ki said, extending his hand. "I use the side of my hand to strike, rather than the knuckles which are easily broken against a man's face."

The reporter studied the samurai's hand. "You mean you chop down like a hatchet like I saw in that room when you broke that man's wrist?"

"Exactly. And there are foot strikes and other blows that I use, always in self-defense."

"I see." The reporter wet the tip of his pencil and mused aloud. "All of which are really not much good against a gun or a knife."

"That is where you are mistaken," Jessie said. "Ki, why don't you show him *atemi*."

The reporter looked from one of them to the other. "Show me what?"

"Better to demonstrate," Ki said, suddenly dropping his hand on the man's shoulder and jabbing his thumb hard into one of the reporter's vital pressure points.

"But . . ."

The man's eyes suddenly rolled up in his head and he toppled forward. The samurai caught him before he crashed face down on the lobby floor, and while guests and the hotel clerk stared, Ki lowered the reporter to a sitting position on the lowest rung of stairs.

26

The reporter looked to be peaceful in sleep as Ki and Jessie went upstairs to their rooms.

Before they separated, Jessie said, "Do you think that we'll have visitors tonight?"

"If they come," Ki said, "I will be ready for them."

Jessie frowned. "I'd rather not have any more trouble. Why don't we just sneak out in the back way in a few minutes and sleep in the livery near our horses. That way, we won't have to worry about anything except catching our train early tomorrow morning."

Ki shrugged his shoulders. He would play this any way that Jessie wanted. Personally, he would not have given up a room already paid for because of the threat of violence. But it was Jessie's money, not his own.

"We're not running away from anything," Jessie said. "It's just that I don't want any more blood spilled."

"All right," Ki said, knowing that he would not sleep anywhere in Denver as long as there was even the remotest chance of trouble. Sleep could wait until they were safely berthed in a private compartment and rolling westward.

Ten minutes later they were packed and slipping down the hallway, then going out the fire escape and down the alley toward the livery. Ki was scowling all the time which prompted Jessie to say, "This doesn't sit too well with you, I know that. But we can't afford to get into trouble here. Not with the Black Bandana Gang terrorizing western Nevada."

"I'll keep reminding myself of that fact," Ki said as they passed through the back streets. "But I hope you haven't forgotten that the miners will guess we are leaving on the Denver Pacific Line tomorrow morning. Hiding out tonight might be just postponing an inevitable showdown."

It was Jessie's turn to frown. "Well," she said, "if that's the case, then at least we'll face those miners well rested."

Chapter 5

In the morning, they awoke rested but Jessie could see that the samurai was worried about the danger she might be in when they arrived at the train depot.

Ki confirmed this impression when he said, "Why don't you let me go ahead early and, if it's all clear, I'll . . ."

"Not on your life," Jessie said, pulling on a coat to hide the sixgun she'd strapped around her hip. "We're sticking together."

There were very few passengers when they arrived at the train depot. It was cold outside and no one was in a talkative mood as Jessie purchased their tickets.

"Train will be leaving right at seven," the ticket master informed them. "Passengers can get on board now."

Jessie looked up at the big clock on the wall. It was a quarter to seven. The train's conductor was sending new passengers down the aisle.

"We might as well board," Jessie said.

As she and Ki handed the conductor their tickets, however, the man whispered, "Miss Starbuck, you and your friend are gonna cause us a whole lot of trouble this morning."

"What's that supposed to mean?"

The conductor glanced up the aisle and dropped his voice

even lower. "You see that man with the black bowler hat?"

"Yes."

"Neither of you turn your back on him, Miss Starbuck. He's a hired gun and he's after you. Might be another one or two in the front cars."

"Thank you!" Jessie said, tipping the man twenty dollars and moving up the aisle.

They took a seat several rows behind the man in the bowler. Jessie was against the window, Ki on the aisle.

"Shall I brace him?" Ki asked quietly.

"No," Jessie said. "Let's just wait and see what he does. We can't make a move against him until he makes one against us."

"Not so," the samurai argued. "Why wait until he pulls a hideout gun from his sleeve and opens fire?"

Jessie didn't have a ready answer to that. "We're in no danger as long as we're behind him. I just wonder if the conductor knew what he was talking about when he said there might be other hired guns in the forward compartments."

"It wouldn't surprise me," Ki said. "Those miners seem to have plenty of money to spend and they're vengeful people. My bet says that they might well have hired a couple of extra gunnies for insurance. We might not uncover them until we're halfway to Nevada."

Jessie had the same uneasy feeling. "We'll just take things one step at a time," she said, studying the man with the bowler hat. "If trouble comes, we'll be ready."

Trouble did not come until their train arrived in Cheyenne. Then, as they were getting ready to disembark and connect with the Union Pacific to Reno, the man in the bowler hat came hurrying down the aisle. Jessie saw him and so did Ki, but since he didn't make a move toward his gun, there was nothing they could do as he shouldered aside other passengers, then pretended to lose his balance and crash into Ki at the very instant the samurai was descending to the railroad platform.

It was obvious to Jessie that the man had timed the collision perfectly. He rammed into Ki so hard that the samurai was very nearly knocked off the steps.

"Hey!" the man shouted, "Watch your goddamn step, Chinaman!"

Ki turned and faced the man.

"I want an apology, damn you!" the man said, pushing his coattails away from his gun butt.

Ki's dark eyes shuttered and Jessie, knowing the samurai was about to strike, said, "Mister, you are the one that owes an apology. Better make it while you still can."

The man in the bowler didn't take his eyes off the samurai. "Lady," he said, "I got no fight with you. Stay out of this."

Jessie's hand went to the sixgun on her hip but in that instant, an unseen assailant behind her brought the barrel of his sixgun crashing down against her skull. Dimly, Jessie heard gunfire and felt herself falling. She heard a woman scream somewhere close at hand and then she lost consciousness as a *shuriken* "star blade" embedded itself into the forehead of the man with the bowler hat.

But as Ki attempted to break Jessie's fall, there was no way he could protect himself from the second assassin's bullets. Realizing that, he shielded Jessie's body and took three bullets, two in the body and one that grazed his skull and sent him sprawling across the platform.

"Say goodbye to this world," the man who'd pistol-whipped Jessie growled as he took careful aim and prepared to put a bullet through Ki's heart.

"Freeze!"

The assassin spun around and started to raise his gun but he had no chance at all. Three bullets stitched into his chest in an area no larger than a silver dollar.

"I told you to freeze," a tall young man with a smoking gun in his fist said with a shake of his head.

The assassin's eyes rolled up into his skull and he fell into the cinders beside the tracks. In the next instant, the tall man was leaping down and checking to see if Jessie was still

30

breathing or if she'd been pistol-whipped so severely that she'd died of brain damage.

Satisfied that Jessie was alive, the man jumped to Ki's side and turned him over to look at his wounds.

"Conductor!" he shouted. "Get my medical bag on the seat where I left it! Hurry!"

The same conductor who had warned Jessie back in Denver now jumped back into the train. He returned in a moment later with the bag.

"Is the Chinaman dead?"

"I don't think he's any more of a Chinaman than we are," the doctor snapped as he tore open his bag, yanked out bandages, and frantically attempted to stem the flow of Ki's blood.

"Down in Denver, they said he was a samurai, whatever the hell that meant," the conductor whispered. He then blurted, "Doc Wells, where the devil did you learn to use a gun like that!"

"Hold this bandage down tight!" the doctor demanded as he examined Ki's head wound. "Is Doctor Calvin still practicing medicine here in Cheyenne?"

"Nope. He died last winter."

"Then . . ."

"There's just old Doc Hanes."

"Damn, he's nothing but a quack! I can't take these people to him."

"Then you might as well treat them yourself. They're going to Reno. You said that you were going all the way to Sacramento, didn't you, Doc?"

"Yeah, but . . ."

"Miss Starbuck will have a first-class coach reserved. Might be the cleanest place you could find to dig the bullet out of that Chinaman. That's it waitin' right over there."

Doc Wells ground his teeth in frustration. He looked up to see the waiting Union Pacific train taking on coal and water.

"How soon is it pulling out?"

The conductor started to raise his hands from the bandage

but thought better of it. Ki had been shot in the side and again high in the chest. If the bullet had missed his lungs then the samurai had a fighting chance.

"What are you going to do, Doc?" the conductor said nervously.

"Let's get them onto the Union Pacific before it pulls out," Wells said. "There's nothing that can help them in this town."

Several passengers were recruited to lift Jessie and Ki and carry them to the Union Pacific train.

"Now wait just a minute," the Union Pacific conductor said. "This no hospital car!"

"Stand aside!" Doc Wells shouted. "These two people have tickets."

"But . . ."

"Stand aside!" the doctor shouted again, louder this time as he drew his own ticket from his pocket.

The conductor's resistance crumbled and someone found Jessie and Ki's tickets.

"First class," the conductor from the Denver Pacific Line crowed. "I told you that's how Miss Starbuck and her friends always travel."

"Show me the way to their coach," the doctor ordered, "and bring me some hot water and plenty of towels."

When Jessie and Ki were laid out on their own berths, Wells removed his coat and reopened his bag as the men who'd carried Jessie and Ki from the train platform to this Union Pacific coach exited.

"Thanks, men," Wells called as they all heard the train's shrill whistle blast a warning.

"Good luck, Doc!" the conductor from the other line shouted at the door.

Doc Wells looked up. "You saw everything that happened. Tell the authorities exactly what transpired. The man I shot would have turned his sixgun on me after he finished off the samurai."

"He sure would have," the conductor agreed. "Good luck, Doc! Your pa would have been even prouder of your gun work than he was of your doctorin'."

Wells nodded. And as he reached for his scalpel and forceps, he was painfully aware that truer words were never spoken. Old Silas Wells had been a gunfighter. As good as they'd come, and he'd shot a lot of men, most of them with bounties on their heads but a few just out of pure contrariness.

Dr. Bill Wells glanced over at Jessie. She was a magnificent woman and he hoped to God that she had not suffered any permanent damage. The man who'd pistol-whipped her hadn't been any too gentle.

The train lurched forward and began to pick up speed. Doc Wells, only two years out of Harvard Medical School, bent over the samurai and took a deep breath. The swaying, jolting coach was going to make his job even more difficult than normal.

The young doctor sleeved a cold sweat from his brow, then he touched the scalpel to Ki's shoulder and widened the incision. Using gauze to soak up the excess blood, he slipped his forceps into the samurai's shoulder and began to probe for the bullet.

For what seemed like an eternity, he leaned forward, trying to steady his hand against the motion of the train and concentrating all of his being on the tips of his forceps. At last, he felt them scrape something hard and he was sure that it wasn't bone.

"Come on, come on!" he whispered.

A moment later, he pinched down hard on the forceps and extracted a misshapen .45 caliber slug. The wound bled even more freely and the young doctor packed it with medicinal powder, then covered it with gauze.

"One down," he said to himself, "one bullet left to go."

He studied Ki's side and biting his lower lip in concentration, he again made a small incision.

"Here, let me help you, Doctor."

Wells looked up suddenly. He'd been concentrating so hard on his work that he'd lost track of time and of the woman beside him.

33

"Are you sure?" he asked, seeing how pale Jessie's face was and how the pupils of her lovely eyes were still a little dilated.

"Yes."

Wells gave her a stack of gauze, then returned his full attention to the wound.

"Who are you?"

"I'm a doctor."

"Are the one that saved Ki's life?"

"I'm trying to, Miss Starbuck. But it would help if I could hold the questions until later."

"I'm sorry."

"So am I," he said. "Gunning down a man is one hell of a poor way for a doctor to uphold his Hippocratic Oath."

"I'm sure that you had no choice."

"We always have a choice," Wells said, closing his eyes so that he could concentrate better on the tips of his forceps.

Jessie watched him very intently. He was about her age and quite handsome. His fingers were long, like his body, but they were anything but clumsy. His hair was blond and wavy, his face too pale, and his eyes a deep blue.

Who are you? she wondered as she stared at the man. *And can you save my best friend?*

"Got it!" Wells cried, pulling out the second slug. "I think he's going to live if we can get the bleeding stopped."

Jessie, despite a terrible pain in her head, smiled. Ki would make it all right. And somehow she would find a way to repay this wonderful, wonderful man.

★

Chapter 6

That evening as their train was rolling down the western slope of the Laramie Mountains, Ki opened his eyes and looked up at Jessie.

"How long have I been unconscious," he asked weakly.

"Only about fourteen hours," Jessie said. "You've lost a lot of blood. The doctor says that you'll be pretty weak for quite some time and you'll have to stay still for a few days until those bullet wounds begin to heal."

Ki looked down at the bandages on his shoulder and side. He winced and reached up to touch his head to feel a third bandage. "Is there any part of me that wasn't shot?"

"A few," Jessie said with a smile. "The important thing is that you're going to be fine."

"You took a pretty good lick yourself across the head, didn't you?"

Jessie nodded. "We were very, very fortunate to get out of this one. There were two gunmen on that train."

"Maybe there are even more," Ki said in warning.

"I don't think so," Jessie said.

Doctor Wells appeared at Jessie's side. "How's the patient?"

"Fine," Ki told him, dimly remembering the gunfire, "thanks to you."

The doctor's smile faded. "I didn't want to kill that man but there wasn't any margin for error so I shot for the heart."

"And you must have hit what you aimed for or I wouldn't be alive to hear about it," Ki said.

"Killing someone, even in a situation like that, is not something that I am particularly happy about," the doctor admitted. "Now, do you mind if I check those wounds?"

The doctor quickly changed Ki's bandages. "They look to be healing properly," he said when he was finished. "And now that you're conscious, I don't think there's any reason why I need to be here."

Dr. Wells turned to Jessie. "Let me take one last look at that scalp wound."

"Ouch!" Jessie said when he touched it gently.

"It is going to be very tender for a few days," the doctor told her. "It's a shame that I had to cut away a little of your beautiful hair."

"It will grow back."

The doctor excused himself saying, "I'll come by first thing tomorrow morning and check on you both."

Jessie smiled. "How about sharing breakfast with us?"

"Delighted," he said as he left their coach.

Ki studied Jessie a moment and then said. "You've got that predatory look in your lovely eyes, Jessie."

She pulled her eyes away from the door. "Predatory? Hardly. It's just that we owe that man our lives."

"I have a feeling that he'll be amply rewarded—if he wants to be."

Jessie blushed a little. "You know me all too well, don't you?"

"Well enough," Ki said, managing a grin despite the discomfort caused by three bullet wounds. "Well enough."

Jessie, Ki, and Dr. Wells had breakfast every morning after that and by the time that they were traveling across Utah Territory, Jessie had learned about the doctor's gunfighting father and how he had vowed to save far more lives than his father had taken.

"It's paying off a debt," Dr. Wells tried to explain late one evening in his private compartment as he and Jessie were gazing out at the Great Salt Lake. "All my life I grew up hearing the legend of my father. Seeing fear in the eyes of grown men when his name was mentioned."

"And you knew."

"Yes. Everyone knew. My father loved the feel and the heft of a gun in his fist, though I don't think he enjoyed killing. He taught me how to handle weapons at an early age."

"You mean how to shoot straight?" Jessie asked. "My father taught me the same."

"I'm sure he did," Wells said, remembering the gun on Jessie's shapely hip. "But I doubt very much that he taught you the fast draw."

"No," Jessie said. "My father was a businessman. Besides, he always said the fast draw probably got more people killed than anything."

"He's right." Wells frowned. "Unless it's practiced constantly, it can be a liability. At least that's what I thought until I put three bullet holes in that man who was about to execute Ki."

"Was your father good to you?"

"Yes. He'd loved my mother very much and when she died, he sort of thought that I carried a part of her. He set aside half of every bounty he ever collected for my education. That's how I was able to go to medical school."

"I see."

"We didn't have a lot of money. It didn't matter. I was raised outside Denver and as long as I had a few friends, a horse, and a dog, I was happy."

Jessie nodded and the doctor's eyes assumed a faraway look. "You see, I lived with my grandparents most of the time. My father would take what he called 'an assignment' and then he'd vanish for anywhere from a week to several months. Sometimes, he'd come back with bullet wounds. Sometimes, he'd just come back with a haunted look."

"So what finally happened?"

"What you'd expect," Wells said. "One time, when I was about sixteen, my father didn't come back at all."

"It must have been very hard."

"It was," Wells said quietly. "I learned later that a murderer that my father had captured somehow managed to grab a girl by the throat. He told my father he'd snap her neck if he didn't hand over his gun."

"And?" Jessie asked when the doctor paused for a long time.

"And the man took my father's gun and killed him. Then he used the girl and let her go. I saw her years later. She said that my father was a very brave man because he'd known that he was about to die and he'd still given up his gun."

Jessie touched the doctor's cheek. "Then you have a wonderful reason to remember him fondly. He might have lived by the gun, but he showed great heroism when the chips were down. My father was very brave too."

Jessie told the doctor about how her mother was killed by the cartel and then her father as well. She ended by saying, "My father, like yours, didn't live as long as he should have, but he left this world a better place. And he left me with a lot of pride in his memory."

There was a long silence as they sat, each remembering their fathers and staring out at the harsh desert with the distant lake. Then Jessie felt his long, supple fingers touch her cheek, and when she turned her face to him, his lips found hers.

His kiss fired her blood and she moved strongly in his arms. "I want you," she breathed as he expertly unbuttoned her dress.

"You've got me," he whispered, removing her clothes and then pausing for a moment to admire her beautiful body. "I've never seen anything to match you, Jessie. Not anatomically or artistically, or any other way."

Jessie smiled and watched as he quickly undressed. He was slender, like Ki, but strong-looking with wide shoulders and narrow hips. His manhood was already stiffening with desire and it was very large.

Jessie lay back on his narrow berth. "I wish that we had a little more room in here. I'd take you into my coach but that would require some adjustments."

He laughed, ducked his head under the overhead luggage rack and slipped in between her legs. Jessie reached down, took his huge rod and guided it to her most private place where she gently rubbed it up and down until her juices were flowing.

"Any time you're ready, Doctor."

He was more than ready. With a growl way down in his throat, young Dr. Wells drove his stiff rod deep into Jessie's lovely body.

"Oh yes," she sighed, opening herself up completely and then reaching down to grip his buttocks so that she could pull him in even farther. "Yes!"

The doctor's hips pistoned in and out, slowly at first, then faster.

"Slow down a little, honey," Jessie panted.

He slowed and they rocked together with the clickity-clacking rhythm of the train as it sped westward over the tracks.

"Can we just stay like this all night," Jessie said, her hips squirming and a fire burning sweetly between her long legs.

"You might be able to," he said breathed, "but I can't."

"Try," she whispered, milking him with her insides and feeling his body respond by moving in and out of her even faster.

"This is the best—by far—I've ever had," he said fervently in her ear.

Jessie held him tight and used the motion of the train to augment her own lovemaking skills. When she felt the doctor begin to twitch and thrash, she knew that he was going to lose control and so she gave herself over to the mounting waves of pleasure she felt lifting her up higher and higher.

Digging her fingers into the flesh of his buttocks and urging him on with desperate lunges and moans, she wrapped her legs around his hips and pleaded, "Come on, Doctor! Give it to me. Give it *all* to me!"

Wells lost control and began to buck and slam his hips against Jessie's causing her to cry out with ecstasy as her own body lost control.

She buried her face in his neck and cried out with pleasure as she felt his hot seed pour into her body. Then she threw her head back and gasped as her hips spasmed and her own juices poured hotly between their legs.

Afterward, they lay in silence, locked in their lovers' embrace. Finally, the doctor raised up a little and gazed down at her in the starlight that poured through their compartment window.

"I'd like to do this again," he said.

"So would I." Jessie laughed. "How about all night long?"

"And every night until we reach Sacramento."

"Ki and I are only going as far as Reno."

"Maybe that's as far as I'll go too."

Jessie shook her head. "There's trouble awaiting us in Nevada. I don't think you want any part of it, Doctor."

"I did pretty well in Cheyenne, didn't I?"

"Yes, you did," Jessie had to admit.

"Well then? My business in Sacramento isn't all that important. In fact, all I'm doing there is visiting a doctor who advertised that he needed a junior partner. The offer sounded good. He wants to retire in a few years and has a very thriving practice."

"So talk to him," Jessie said.

"I'd rather spend more time with you in Nevada," he said, bumping his hips against hers.

Jessie stroked his smooth flanks and when he lowered his head and began to use his tongue on her lush breasts, she did not have the will to try and persuade him not to stay with her awhile in Nevada.

"Yes," she said with a sigh as he again buried his long, wet rod in her honeypot, "maybe you should come with us to Carson City."

The doctor grunted an agreement and, after that, words seemed inappropriate considering what their bodies were frantically telling them.

★

Chapter 7

The railroad trip across western Utah and northern Nevada was amorously eventful for Jessie and Doc Wells and by the time they arrived in Reno, Ki's wounds were beginning to mend.

"Have you decided what you want to do?" Jessie asked the doctor as the train began to unload.

"I'm coming with you," Doc Wells said. "From what you've confided about the Black Bandana Gang, their kidnapping, looting and murdering, I think my services might be better appreciated here than in Sacramento."

Secretly, Jessie was pleased. She was not in love with the handsome young doctor, but she was quite infatuated with him. Besides, he was not only an excellent doctor that could keep a watchful eye to make sure that Ki's wounds healed properly, but he was very courageous and skilled with a sixgun.

Ki moved stiffly as they disembarked and hailed a carriage that would take them to the Holiday House located beside the Truckee River. After obtaining rooms and making certain that Ki was resting comfortably, Jessie prepared herself to pay a visit to the Reno sheriff's office.

"May I come along?" Doc Wells inquired.

Jessie took her lover's arm. "Of course."

Sheriff Douglas Commer leaned back in his swivel chair and regarded his scuffed boots resting on his scarred office desk. He was pushing fifty, a balding, self-important man, tall with a sunken chest and a little pot belly that drooped over his gunbelt. He had an annoying habit of scratching himself in immodest places and spitting chewing tobacco before almost every sentence he uttered. His teeth and his shirt were both stained a dark, beetle-brown, and even at arms length he exuded a rank smell.

"So what you're asking me," he said, regarding Jessie with a mixture of lust and distrust, "is if I think the Black Bandana Gang is hiding out in my jurisdiction."

"That's right," Jessie said, having trouble hiding her dislike for this man.

"The answer is no, I do not. If I thought they were in my jurisdiction, I'd hunt them down and arrest them."

"Then where do you think they are hiding?"

"Miss Starbuck, if I knew that answer to that question, I'd be a fool to tell you. You see, there's a ten-thousand-dollar reward for information on that gang. I could use that kind of money."

Jessie frowned. "Then you really have nothing to tell me of any value."

The sheriff dropped his boots to the floor. "Oh, now, I didn't say that. I have lots of valuable things I'd like to tell you, now, or maybe tonight over dinner."

"Not a chance," Jessie said. "We're leaving for Carson City."

"Too bad," the sheriff drawled. "But I'd like to give you a piece of free advice—just do whatever pretty rich women do and stay the hell out of the business of catching outlaws. This so-called Black Bandana Gang is likely no more than a bunch of cutthroats that have been a little lucky as of late. They'll get caught sooner or later but it will be by the *law*, Miss Starbuck. Not by you."

Jessie felt her cheeks warm. "Sheriff," she said tightly, "they murdered one of my father's dearest old friends— Judge Milton Archibald. And they most likely did it out of revenge for someone the judge sentenced either to prison or to a hanging."

"Yeah, probably," Commer said, spitting and missing his cuspidor. "But I got my own hunches and theories about all this."

Jessie sighed. Curiosity made her ask, "What hunches and theories?"

"What about dinner?"

Beside her, Doc Wells growled, "You're supposed to be a professional lawman—not an over-the-hill lecher. If you've got some light to shed, then do it and stop bothering the lady!"

Sheriff Commer jumped to his feet, his face mottled with anger. "Just who the hell do you think you are! This is my office and I damn sure don't need some wet-behind-the-ears sawbones telling me what I can do or say."

Wells balled his fists and if Jessie had not stepped between the two men, she was sure that the young doctor would have battered the disgusting sheriff senseless.

"Stop it!" she said. "Bill, let's get out of here. This so-called sheriff isn't going to give us any answers."

"Oh yeah!" Commer shouted as they moved to the door. "Well I think this whole Black Bandana Gang is pure hocum! I don't think there is such a gang! I think it was all made up by some newspaper reporters trying to come up with a good story!"

Jessie whirled around at the door. "If that's true, who killed my friend Judge Archibald? And who took those two young people who were in his house at the time of his murder and what did they do with them?"

Sheriff Commer's shoulder's sagged a little and the heat washed out of him. "I dunno," he confessed. "But maybe there really isn't a gang. Maybe it's just a bunch of sonsabitches each killin' and raisin' hell all on their own and the only thing they got in common is that they all wear black bandanas."

The sheriff sneered. "You ever think of *that*, Miss Starbuck?"

Instead of answering, Jessie just wheeled around on her boot heels and headed outside.

Wells caught her a moment later and, falling in beside her with his long stride, said, "What did you think about the sheriff's theory?"

"It's possible," Jessie conceded. "In fact, if there were no single gang, as he suggests, then it would explain why the authorities haven't had any success."

"So what now?"

"We leave for Carson City first thing tomorrow morning," Jessie said.

Carson City was sharing in the enormous prosperity being generated on the Comstock Lode less than thirty miles away. It was the state capital and before that had been the territorial capital of Nevada. Stamping mills to process Comstock ore and lumber mills to cut timber for the deep mines were the major sources of employment for the people of Carson City, although freighting and agriculture were also keys to a thriving economy.

The capitol, with its high-domed roof, was impressive and so were the tree-shaded grounds. Jessie, Ki, and Doc Wells took separate rooms at the plush Ormsby House.

When they were settled, Jessie announced that she was going to visit the local sheriff.

"I want to come along," Wells said.

"Me too," Ki echoed.

But Jessie shook her head at the samurai. "I want you to stay here and recover. Those bullet wounds could easily reopen."

Ki said nothing, but it was easy to see by his expression that he was anything but pleased.

"Jessie is right," the doctor said. "You came within a hair's width of being killed."

Jessie moved over and sat down on the samurai's bed. "There's another reason why it would be better if you didn't come today," she said.

"And that is?"

"If there is some kind of conspiracy in northern Nevada, I think it would be more valuable if you were not linked with me."

"But . . ."

Jessie cut off his protest with her fingertips. "Ki, you'll be well soon and if you can operate detached from me and Bill, then I think you might have more opportunity to help us get to the bottom of this. Right now, no one really knows that I'm in town or for what purpose. There isn't a link between me and Judge Archibald. Not yet, anyway."

Jessie leaned back. "Don't you see how this could work out much better? We could be working independently, yet be in constant touch and sharing information."

"But if I'm not beside you, your life will be in greater danger."

"I know," Jessie admitted. "But there's also the thought that, the sooner we find out who is behind the judge's murder and if those two hostages are still alive, the sooner we'll all be finished here. I do have a business meeting in San Francisco in ten days, and with luck, we can solve this mystery and be on our way."

Ki nodded with reluctance. He looked to the doctor. "How long before I can practice my fighting skills?"

"A week. No sooner."

Ki and Jessie exchanged glances. Jessie knew that the samurai would not wait even four days before he would be up and about. What the doctor did not understand was that the samurai was not an ordinary physical specimen. His body was perfectly conditioned and he had a remarkable ability to recover from injury.

"Let's go," Jessie said. "It's almost five o'clock and I want to catch the sheriff before he closes up for the evening."

Sheriff Pace Malloy was young, smart, and everything good that his counterpart in Reno was not. Of average size and looks, he had penetrating brown eyes and a quick, boyish smile that could not hide the fact that he was ambitious and serious about upholding the law.

"I've only been sheriff for two weeks," he told them right from the start. "I was hired after the last sheriff was shot to death."

"By the Black Bandana Gang?" Jessie asked quickly.

"That's the general opinion," Pace said. "When I was hired there was such a state of fear going on around here that the governor himself came in for the interview and when the mayor pinned on my badge, they both assured me that, in the event I was also murdered, my wife and two small children would receive a very generous pension."

Jessie shook her head. "That must have been a little unnerving."

"It was," Malloy admitted. "I'd been the sheriff in Virginia City and that's a rough town to ride herd on, but this Black Bandana Gang thing has everyone about half spooked out of their socks."

"Do you have any leads to the murder of Judge Archibald or the disappearance of those two young people from his house?"

"Not yet, but I'm working on it," Malloy said. "Are you aware that we have the state prison right outside town?"

"Yes. But what . . ."

"Could be that this gang business starts right out there."

"What makes you say that?" Doc Wells asked.

Malloy scratched behind his ear. "I've just heard things. Rumors."

"Could you be more specific?" Jessie asked.

"I'm afraid not," the young sheriff said almost apologetically. "You see, there's an inmate out there that sort of owes me his life. He was drunk and was the survivor of a vicious knife fight. The friends of the dead man said that he was attacked. Others said that both men freely entered the fight and were drunk."

Jessie nodded and held her silence as the sheriff continued.

"At any rate, despite previous convictions, I spoke to the court before sentencing and got the judge to give my informant prison instead of the rope. He made some mistakes, but I didn't think he deserved to die for this particular stabbing. I was convinced that it was a matter of self-defense."

"And he's supplying you with information on the Black Bandana Gang?"

Malloy shook his head. "So far he's too afraid to give me any names. But I told him that if he helps me solve this thing it would go a long way to getting him a parole in a few years. Of course, if anyone out there knew that he was working with me, he'd be a dead man."

"Of course," Jessie said. "And I understand why you'd be reluctant to put the man in any situation of risk. But at the same time, you might need someone like us to help."

Malloy grinned. "No offense, Miss Starbuck. I've heard your name and know that your father was quite a man. But you'll have to understand that I'm not going to count too much on a woman and a doctor. I'm the law in this town now, and this is my problem, not yours."

Jessie curbed her anger because the last thing she wanted to do was to get into an argument with this young lawman. "Sheriff," she said, "if it's the credit you're after, have no fear. We don't even want our names mentioned. However . . ."

"Miss Starbuck," Malloy said in a clipped voice, "Doc Wells, enjoy your stay in Carson City but leave this Black Bandana thing up to a professional. And now, I think we've finished our little chat and I've more than enough work to do."

Jessie was not accustomed to being dismissed. "Just one thing I ask."

Malloy, who had began to shuffle papers on his desk, looked up. "Yes, ma'am?"

"If, at any point, this thing seems to be getting out of hand for you, please promise me that you'll seek our help."

"It won't 'get out of hand.' "

"But if it does," Jessie insisted. "All I ask is that you remember us and don't be too stubborn or proud to seek help."

47

Pace Malloy could see that Jessie would not budge until he agreed to her request so he nodded. "All right. I promise. Now, will you let me get back to work?"

"Of course," Jessie said, forcing a smile. "And thank you for your time."

Outside, Jessie and Wells strolled along the boardwalk and entered the tree-filled capitol grounds.

"You haven't said a single word since we left Malloy's office," the doctor observed. "A penny for your thoughts."

Jessie spotted a bench off by itself and went to it. Taking a seat, she crossed her legs and watched a hawk soar overhead.

"I'm afraid that Sheriff Malloy, while a man of high ideals and ambitions, is in a bit over his head. And, unfortunately, he'll be too proud to ask for help despite his promise."

"So what can we do?" Wells asked. "We can't make the man come to us."

Jessie laced her fingers behind her head and continued to watch the hawk soar lazily on the updrafting air currents that followed the slopes of the eastern Sierras.

"The sheriff said he testified in court in behalf of a man that would otherwise have hanged because he stabbed another man to death in a fight. I am sure that if we went up to Virginia City and paid a visit to their courthouse someone ought to be able to tell us the name of the man in question."

Doc Wells allowed himself the barest hint of a smile. "You're probably right."

Jessie got up. "But we have to be very, very careful. Malloy is right. If we somehow let it be known to the wrong people that this prisoner was cooperating with either ourselves or Malloy, he's a dead man."

Doc Wells fell in beside Jessie. "All right," he said, thinking aloud. "So what if we do figure out the name of this prisoner? How do we approach him if he's locked behind bars?"

"I don't know yet," Jessie admitted. "But I have learned that you take these kinds of things one small step at a time. First the name, then we worry about how to reach him."

"Why would he talk to you?" the doctor asked. "The sheriff has done him a favor and could do him another by helping him get an early parole. What can you offer?"

"Money," Jessie said. "I can offer him enough money so that if he does get that parole he'll never have to work again in his lifetime."

"You'd pay him that much?"

"To get to the bottom of who murdered Judge Archibald and abducted his help? Of course I would."

"So where are we going right now?"

Jessie looked up at the sun as it dove toward the crest of the nearby Sierras. "If I recall," she said, "the Virginia & Truckee Railroad leaves for the Comstock every morning. We'll be on the train and in the Virginia City courthouse before noon. With a little luck, we should be back here by tomorrow evening."

"You work very fast, don't you?" the doctor said, taking her arm.

Jessie batted her pretty eyelashes. "You ought to know, Doctor, you ought to know."

He chuckled. "Tonight after dinner?"

"Of course," Jessie said, unable to hide her anticipation of another night of lovemaking.

★

Chapter 8

Early the next morning, Jessie stopped by to visit the samurai and tell him of her plans. When she was finished, Ki frowned.

"What's the matter?" Jessie asked.

"It just that if you ask many questions up there, it might raise suspicions."

"Do you know of a better way to find out who the prisoner is that Sheriff Malloy thinks can and will help him?"

"No," Ki said. "But if you do find out the prisoner's name, then you're going to need someone to reach him. You can't just expect him to spill what he might know to strangers."

Jessie's eyes narrowed. "What are you saying?"

"I'm saying that I'm the only one that could survive inside that prison and find out what he, or any other inmates know about the Black Bandana Gang."

Jessie paled a little. "We've visited the Texas State Prison. You know as well as I do what it's like inside those places."

"Sure," Ki said agreeably. "But all I'm saying is that if there is no other way then I will go inside."

Jessie stood up quickly. She did not even want to think of what would happen to Ki inside a prison if anyone even suspected he was a plant. Not even the skilled samurai would have a chance at remaining alive under those circumstances. The prisoners called plants "stooges" and would kill them.

"Just mend quickly," Jessie said on her way out the door. "With any luck at all, Doc Wells and I should be back by this evening with the name of Sheriff Malloy's prisoner friend."

"If Malloy ever realizes we've gone around him, he'll be fit to be tied," the samurai observed. "We could make a pretty important enemy in that man."

"I know, but what else can we do if he's unwilling to accept our offer of help?"

When Ki couldn't answer, Jessie left him and went downstairs to meet the doctor. Together, they walked to the old roundhouse station a few blocks east of town where they bought tickets and rode the Virginia & Truckee Railroad up to Virginia City.

Jessie had ridden the train several times before, and she always found it enjoyable. The little narrow-gauge track wound up through the sun-blasted and sage-covered foothills east of town to snake up through the canyons to the Comstock. Because it was a continuous uphill climb, the ride took nearly three hours and there were too many sharp switchbacks to count. But at last, the little train hauled itself over the final divide and then rolled past the huge Fourth Ward Schoolhouse and St. Mary of the Mountains Catholic Church into the depot.

Wells had never seen such a booming metropolis, but he was not one bit impressed with the harsh, treeless mountainsides.

"They couldn't have picked a more desolate place to discover ore, could they?" he said.

"I suppose not," Jessie replied. "And it must have seemed especially inhospitable up here considering that so many of the Comstock miners came over the Sierras after the California gold strikes finally played out."

"Where do they get water? I see no sign of any lakes or rivers."

"They pump it over those hills up from Washoe Lake to the west. And they have built several reservoirs. It snows pretty hard up here in the wintertime."

"I can see that," the doctor said, pointing to the summit of Sun Mountain where snow lay in the shadows of rocks.

"Come on," Jessie said, taking the doctor's hand. "We've got to hike all the way up to A Street where the Storey County Courthouse is located."

The doctor shook his head. The hike was a steep and a long one. "I'm not sure that I'm in shape for this."

"Of course you are," Jessie said, pulling him along.

It took five minutes to climb up to C Street, Virginia City's main thoroughfare. "My heavens," Wells panted, trying to catch his breath in the thin, high-desert air. "How many saloons are there in this city?"

"At least fifty," Jessie said. "Bucket of Blood, Delta, and the Silver Queen are the most popular. But there are a lot more that remain packed twenty-four hours a day."

When they finally struggled up to C Street, they turned left and passed the Knights of Pythias and its close neighbor, the Miners Union halls. Crossing Sutton Street, they heard the piano music and someone shouting instructions to a company of dancers.

"What's this?" Doc Wells asked, hesitating before a huge brick building.

"Piper's Opera House," Jessie said. "They import talent from all over the country such as the great Shakespearian actor, Edwin Booth, Buffalo Bill Cody, and the famous Lilly Langtry. They've got a huge dance floor that actually sits on railroad springs. When the floor is packed with wild miners, that floor will rock and bounce like the deck of a ship fighting a raging sea."

The doctor's face reflected his astonishment. "Who'd have imagined they'd have culture in a place like this."

"Wherever you have lots of people with lots of money, there's very little that you won't find," Jessie told the doctor. "But we've no time to sightsee today. And right up ahead is the county courthouse."

52

Despite the coolness of the day, they were both perspiring from their climb by the time they entered the huge, two-storied courthouse made of white stone. Their heels clicked loudly as they walked across the polished wood floor.

They came to a halt before a long polished counter and waited as perhaps five or six young men behind desks wearing white shirts and black ties labored over various ledgers and record books.

Surprisingly, it was Doc Wells who lost his patience first. "Ah-hem!" he humphed, loudly clearing his throat to gain attention. "Would one of you chaps please take a moment to help us?"

A harried-looking clerk with sandy-colored hair and thick spectacles jumped to his feet. He hurried over to the counter. "I am sorry," he apologized. "It's just that the county has changed the jurisdictional lines and it has completely messed up the tax rolls. Our accounting system is in chaos and I'm afraid it will be for . . ."

"Quite all right," Jessie said, warming the young clerk with a smile that would have melted an arctic glacier. "We need to speak to someone who is familiar with the criminal cases."

"Ah, the criminal cases!" The clerk brightened. "Well, that certainly doesn't concern us, now does it."

"I shouldn't think so," Jessie said.

"Now," the clerk said, leaning forward and gazing with longing into her clear, green eyes, "let me see. Criminal matters. Yes, that would be upstairs, second door on the right. Mr. Patterson is our bailiff and he can direct you to whomever it is you need. Now, if Mr. Patterson cannot answer all your questions to satisfaction, please return to me and I will personally . . ."

"Thanks," Jessie's young doctor said shortly, cutting the clerk off in midsentence, "but I'm sure that we'll make out just fine upstairs."

He took Jessie's arm and hurried her away.

"Really," Jessie said, pulling her arm free, "there was no reason to be so abrupt with that young fellow."

"He was wasting our time," the doctor said, as they mounted the stairs. "His eyes were as big as saucers and, given another minute or two, he'd have begun to slobber all over the counter."

Jessie suppressed a chuckle. It seemed that Dr. Wells had a streak of jealousy in him.

When they found Mr. Patterson, however, there was nothing for Dr. Wells to be jealous about. Patterson was a large, overweight man with three chins and a perpetual five o'clock shadow. He had beetle brows and a lantern jaw. Jessie's first impression of him was unfavorable, but the man proved to be quite accommodating.

"We're doing a little reporting for an eastern newspaper about how sheriffs can sometimes actually be friends with the very men they arrest," Jessie began. "And I understand this happens all the time in a court of law such as this."

"Not all the time," the bailiff said, "but sometimes, when a sheriff brings in a man that is, well, more naughty than mean, he'll ask the judge for some leniency."

Jessie nodded. "What about something a little more serious than being 'naughty'?"

"What do you mean?"

"Oh, for example my friend and I understand that when Sheriff Pace Malloy was sheriff up here he once saved a man's life even though he'd stabbed another man to death in a knife fight."

The bailiff frowned and rolled his eyes for a moment as both Jessie and the doctor held their breath.

"You mean," the bailiff said slowly, "that time about two years ago when Ferrell Taggert stabbed John Beman to death?"

"Yes," Jessie said, "I think that was the one. The way I understand it, the judge would most certainly have sentenced Taggert to hang if it hadn't been for Sheriff Malloy's intercession."

"That's right enough," the bailiff said, "but I think Malloy made a bad mistake. Even though they say it was a fair fight, Taggert is a mean sonofa . . ." the man caught himself.

54

"I'm sorry miss, but Taggert is a bad one. He'd killed men before and he was always looking for a fight. They say he's as good a man with a knife as there is. Bet he kills a bunch of them inmates down at the prison and I say, good riddance to the bunch of them!"

"Me too," Jessie said, certain now that she had the right name of Malloy's Carson City Prison plant.

"What does this Taggert fella look like?" Dr. Wells asked, showing that he was thinking hard.

"Oh, Taggert is a big man, taller than me and heavier too. I sure was glad to get him out of here. I didn't trust him for a second, not even when he was shackled hand and foot. Taggert has that . . . how would you call it? That coyote look in his eyes. He's cunning and treacherous."

"How long was his sentence?" Jessie asked.

"Twenty-five years and he got off real easy," Patterson said. "Why, he carved that poor fella up like a Thanksgiving turkey. He even cut the man's throat like he was a buck he wanted to bleed out! Now that kind of a man deserves to die."

"He sure does," Jessie agreed. "But you can't sentence a man to death for fighting in self-defense, no matter how heinous the act of killing."

"I don't know what no 'heinous' means, miss, but he slit the poor bastard's throat after he'd already killed him! Now that ought to tell you something about Ferrell Taggert."

"It does," Jessie agreed.

"Say," the bailiff said, "aren't either one of you going to write any of this down? I mean, I want you to keep the facts straight."

Jessie and the doctor started to leave. "We promise, we'll keep the facts straight."

"But," the bailiff called, hurrying after them, "I got lots of other stories about Malloy and other sheriffs who showed a little mercy now and then."

"We'll come back some other time," Jessie called over her shoulder as they were hurrying downstairs.

"Well, don't go and mispell my damned name! It's P-A-T-T-E-R-S-O-N. Two t's and it's an S-O-N at the end, not an S-E-N. You got that!"

"We do, we do!" Dr. Wells called up the staircase as they hurried across the lower lobby and out toward the front door.

The little sandy-haired clerk, however, was lying in wait for them. "Excuse me, did you find out what you wanted to know from Mr. Patterson?" he asked eagerly.

"We sure did," Jessie said.

The clerk could not hide his disappointment. "Well, if there is anything else . . ."

"There isn't," Dr. Wells snapped as he hurried Jessie out of the courthouse.

Once outside, they both relaxed.

"So," the doctor said, "now that we have the prisoner's name, what do we do with it?"

"I'm not sure," Jessie said, thinking about Ki's offer to go into the prison and meet the vicious knife fighter. "I thought I might write the prisoner a letter offering a sizable amount of cash if he would meet and talk with me about the Black Bandana Gang."

"I think that's a bad idea," the doctor said. "He'd either dismiss the letter as being from a quack, or he'd be too afraid to answer for fear of retaliation."

"Then what if I talked to the warden and arranged a meeting?"

Again, the doctor shook his head. "If you did that, the man might as well wear a flag telling his fellow prisoners that he's cooperating with the authorities. He'd never be that stupid."

Jessie frowned. "I'm afraid that you're right. So what does that leave us?"

"You have to get a plant inside the prison," the doctor said. "Someone you could trust to make contact with Ferrell Taggert and somehow get him to tell whatever he knows about the Black Bandana Gang."

"That would be a very, very risky thing."

56

"That's right," the doctor said. "It would take a man with great courage and resourcefulness. A man like myself."

"What!"

The doctor looked offended. "Well, who else did you have in mind?"

"Ki," she blurted. "He's already volunteered."

"But he's shot up!" Wells exclaimed. "He took three bullets and almost bled to death in Cheyenne, or are you forgetting that?"

"Of course I'm not forgetting!" Jessie retorted angrily. "But he's mending and we can wait a week or so before he goes in. Of course, this won't be possible without the warden's cooperation."

"I'm healthy and I'm the one that should be going in there," the doctor complained.

"No offense," Jessie said, "and while I appreciate your great courage, the samurai is better trained to survive than yourself or anyone else I've ever known. He'll find out what we need to know and then he'll find a way to get the information back to us."

The doctor tried to hide the fact that he was secretly relieved. "Whatever you say. But in the meantime, what are we supposed to do while Ki buddies up to this murderous knife fighter?"

"We keep turning over rocks looking for clues to who is behind this vicious gang that killed Judge Archibald. And we also try to find those two young people that were kidnapped."

"Do you really think that there's any chance they are still alive?"

"No," Jessie said quietly, "but we have to try anyway."

Dr. Wells nodded with sad agreement as they started to hike their way back down the Virginia City train depot.

★

Chapter 9

That evening, Jessie, Ki, and Dr. Wells spent several hours discussing their next move. Mostly, the samurai listened to the other two but finally, he had heard enough.

"All this talk is useless," he told them. "Someone has to go into that prison and be placed in the same cell with this Ferrell Taggert. And that someone is me."

Jessie shook her head emphatically. "But you're just not physically strong enough for that yet, Ki."

"She's right," Wells said. "If you were to get into a fight with this man, if he pulled a makeshift blade on you and you had to defend yourself, you'd be nearly helpless."

Ki shook his head. "That's not true," he said stubbornly. "I could even hide my weapons in my tunic and . . ."

"You're forgetting," Jessie interrupted, "that you'd be a prisoner and have to have your head shaved and your civilian clothes taken away."

"I can easily sew a couple of *shuriken* star blades into the prison uniform," Ki argued. "And even with these wounds, I am still a master of *te*. And I am *ninja*."

"What?" the doctor asked.

"The invisible assassin," Ki explained.

"Well," the doctor said, "you can't assassinate anyone through prison bars. You'll be locked in a little cell most

58

of the time. And even when you're out of the cell, you'll be under surveillance every moment."

"I'm still the only man that can do the job," Ki said, looking to Jessie.

She nodded in reluctant agreement. "But not for a few more days until you're a little stronger. Agreed?"

"All right," Ki said.

"Besides," Jessie said, "I've got to find someone in this town who has a strong pull on the warden."

"What about the mayor?" Ki asked. "You met him the last time we were through."

"No," Jessie said, "I need someone whose political career is not on the line if we mess this up." She frowned in concentration. "I need one of Judge Archibald's dearest and most trusted friends."

"And that would be?"

"Judge Joe Davis," Jessie said, remembering the man's stern face. "He's one of the most influential men in Nevada and my father once gave him a huge political contribution. He'll remember and honor that debt."

"How can you be so sure?" Wells asked skeptically.

"I can't," Jessie admitted, "but what do we have to lose by approaching the man and asking for his help?"

"Nothing," Ki said. "Start at the top and work your way down. If nothing else, I can always commit some crime punishable by a mandatory prison sentence."

"No!" both Jessie and Wells echoed.

Ki smiled. "Just testing you," he said innocently as he leaned back in bed and closed his eyes in preparation for sleep.

"Come on," Jessie said to her doctor. "I think we had also better get some sleep."

Out in the hallway, the doctor took her into his arms and said, "Are you sure you want to sleep tonight?"

"Yes," Jessie said, gently pushing him away. "We've had some very good nights together but, from now on, people's lives are at stake and I want to be clearheaded and ready for whatever might go wrong."

Wells didn't like to, but he had to nod his head in agreement. "All right," he said, "business before pleasure."

Jessie smiled warmly, kissed him on the cheek and went to her room. She was tired and tomorrow was going to be very important. She just hoped and prayed that Judge Joe Davis was a man who honored past favors.

At nine o'clock the following morning, Jessie and Dr. Wells knocked on Judge Davis's door. After a few moments, a pleasant looking woman in her sixties appeared.

"Can I help you?"

Jessie introduced herself and the doctor, then said, "We'd like very much to see the judge this morning."

The woman frowned. "He really doesn't like to be disturbed at this hour. He's working in his study but he does have office hours and . . ."

"I understand," Jessie said, "but if you'd tell him that I am Alex Starbuck's daughter and I must see him at once, perhaps he will make an exception and allow us to visit him for a few moments."

"Very well," the woman said, turning back into the hallway. "I'll be right back."

Jessie and Wells waited impatiently and they could hear voices down the hallway. After several minutes, the judge appeared, looking much older than Jessie had remembered. He was bent and rather thin, but she would have recognized his voice and those sharp, probing eyes anywhere.

"Well now! Come in, come! How good it is to see you after all these many years."

Jessie shook hands with the old man and introduced the doctor. Looking at them both, the judge said, "Let me guess, Doctor, you and Jessica are going to be married and you wish me to have the honor of officiating."

Dr. Wells blushed deeply. "I'm afraid that is not the case."

The judge's smile faded. "Then is there some trouble?"

Jessie touched the judge's arm. "Could we talk for a few minutes? It's a matter of some urgency."

"Of course." The judge led them back to his study. It was

60

a small room lined floor to ceiling with books. In the center of the room was a huge oak desk and leather chair. There were papers scattered all over the desk and the entire room had a comfortable, cluttered appearance.

"Excuse my messiness," the judge said. "I have been asked to write my memoirs for the Nevada State Historical Society. They're to be called, 'Thirty Years on the Silver State Bench' or some such nonsense. They want me to write about my most difficult and challenging decisions."

"I'm sure that you will be doing future generations of Nevadans a real service."

"I don't know about that at all," the judge grumbled. "I'm not a natural writer. I struggle over every damned word and, at my age, I often can't recall the details. Fortunately, I've kept a sort of legal diary right from the beginning. But even so, the writing is a toil for me."

The judge winked. "Frankly, I'd rather go fishing."

Jessie smiled. "I'm sure that you will soon. And it's important that historical accounts be written for those who follow us."

The judge nodded. His hand, which Jessie noticed shook slightly, passed lightly across his scattered papers and then he looked directly at her. "Did your father keep any kind of . . ."

"No," Jessie said. "Not even a diary or a daily ledger. He was so busy with everything, all I have left is a few letters that were returned to me by his dearest friends. One of them is yours."

"Yes," the judge said with a sad shake of his head. "I remember. But what brings you to Carson City?"

"The Black Bandana Gang," Jessie said. "I was at Circle Star when I read about how they murdered our dear, mutual friend, Judge Milton Archibald. Ki and I decided that we wanted to see the guilty punished, if they haven't already been."

"No," the judge said, "they have not. I'm afraid this gang—if they are a gang—has the authorities completely baffled."

"Were the two young people who were abducted ever found?"

"The piano tuner's body was discovered just yesterday. At least, they think it is his body. It was pretty badly decomposed. There was no identification except perhaps from the dentistry. The young man's dentist has been sent for but we've just learned he has moved to Sacramento. So it might be a week or more before we have any positive identification."

Jessie shook her head. "But the girl might be still alive?"

"It is possible, but not probable," the judge said, a trace of bitterness in his voice. "Her name is Alice Reynolds. She is just twenty-one and . . . and my own niece."

"I'm sorry," Jessie said.

The judge nodded. "She's a lovely girl. Her father died when she was quite young and her mother has had a real struggle. Alice is a hard worker. She was saving her money to go off to an eastern finishing school. She wanted to better her lot and I was behind her all the way. She would have gone back to Boston this next spring. It was all she talked about."

"Don't lose hope," Jessie said. "She might well be alive."

"I tried to tell myself that," the judge said, "but when they found the boy's body . . ."

The judge was so overcome with emotion he could not speak for several moments, causing Jessie to say, "Perhaps it would be better if Dr. Wells and I came back later."

"No," said the judge, taking a deep breath. "But what you have to understand, Jessica, is that these people, whoever they are, are utterly without conscience. They murder, rob, pillage, and intimidate."

"And the authorities cannot do a thing?"

"They're working on it," the judge said without optimism. "But what is beginning to become obvious is that the gang splinters and often attacks on several different fronts simultaneously. For example, they might rob a bank on the Comstock at the very same time they do a stage holdup just a few miles out of town."

"But wouldn't you expect then that they have a single leader who is planning these forays?"

"Yes, I would."

"Judge," Jessie said. "Sheriff Pace Malloy tells us that there is an inmate in the state prison here who might be willing to break this case wide open, provided he has some hope of an early parole."

The judge suddenly leaned forward. "Oh? And who might that be?"

Jessie and the doctor exchanged glances. "Ferrell Taggert."

Judge Davis's bushy gray eyebrows shot up and his voice hardened. "He's not to be trusted. He'd say anything, even turn in his own mother, if he thought it would lessen his sentence by a single day."

Dr. Wells said, "Sheriff Malloy is hoping he will tell the truth this time. It's our only hope."

"Ki is here," Jessie said. "I'm sure you remember him."

"Of course. The samurai."

"Yes," Jessie said. "And he is willing to go inside the prison and make contact with Taggert."

"He would be foolish indeed to do such a thing."

"No," Jessie argued. "He is a man who could find out what Taggert knows and then escape with his life. All that is required is that you speak to the prison's warden and make the arrangements."

"No," the judge said. "I can't do that. If something went wrong, Ki would be crucified in that place. He'd be tortured, Jessica. It's just too risky—not to mention against the law."

"Is there a law against planting a man inside prison?"

"Of course," the judge said. "It's called 'false imprisonment' and both myself and the state could be sued if Ki were hurt."

Jessie sighed. "Please," she said, "Ki is my best friend. If I thought, even for a moment, that his life would be lost in this endeavor, then I'd never have asked you to speak with the warden."

But the judge shook his head. "I just can't do it," he said. "It's illegal and it's wrong."

Jessie and the doctor knew that there was nothing more that they could say or do to change the judge's mind.

"I guess we'd better be leaving so that you can go back to those memoirs," Jessie said, rising.

"To hell with them!" the judge snapped. "With my niece missing, I can't even sleep at night, much less think about writing."

For the next few minutes, they talked about lighter matters. The weather, the state of the Nevada economy, even about trout fishing, which was the judge's lifelong passion.

And then just as Jessie and Dr. Wells were about to excuse themselves, there came a loud knock on his front door.

"Judge!" a familiar voice called. "Judge Davis!"

The judge came to his feet. "That sounds like Sheriff Malloy calling. I'd better go out to see what is wrong."

They followed the judge back down the narrow hallway to the front door where a very agitated young sheriff was waiting.

"Judge," he blurted, "there's just been another stage holdup and a killing."

Judge Davis's mouth crimped at the corners. "Any deaths?"

"Three. The driver and two shotgun guards. They were all ambushed with rifles and never had a chance. The passengers, thank heavens, were only robbed and none were murdered."

"Thank God," the judge whispered. "But why . . ."

"It's your niece," the sheriff interrupted. "One of the passengers said that she recognized her."

"What!"

"That's right." Sheriff Malloy's face was hard. "The witness said that Alice was helping the gang."

"That's impossible!"

Sheriff Malloy shrugged his shoulders. "She was identi-

64

fied by more than one passenger, Judge. I think we have to assume that they weren't all mistaken."

The judge reached out to grab the doorframe for support, and Dr. Wells reacted quickly to help him back down the hallway where he was gently seated in his leather chair.

Dr. Wells took the old judge's pulse and called for water. When Mrs. Davis saw her husband, she paled.

"He's going to be just fine," the doctor promised. "He's just had a bit of a shock."

The judge looked up at his wife who knelt by his side. "They say that Alice is alive, but she's helping that gang!"

"No!"

"I'm afraid so," Sheriff Malloy said grimly. "She was identified."

Mrs. Davis opened her mouth to speak but no words came.

Dr. Wells, who never traveled without his medical kit, quickly gave both the old people something to calm their emotions.

"I'd better stay with them for a few hours," Wells said to Jessie.

"Good idea."

Just before she left the room, the judge feebly raised his hand and motioned Jessie to his side. Apparently not wanting Sheriff Malloy to overhear what he had to say, the judge whispered, "I'll help you with the warden after all."

"Thank you!"

"But God help Ki if he's found out," the judge whispered in a fervent tone of voice.

Jessie understood all too well what the judge was saying.

Outside, Sheriff Malloy said, "What are you and the doctor doing here?"

"Visiting an old friend of my father's. I remember the judge quite fondly. Is that all right, Sheriff?"

"Well of course. It's just that I like to keep abreast of what's going on in my town."

"I understand," Jessie said. "And I am curious why you

65

aren't forming a posse and going after the gang."

Sheriff Malloy blushed. "The gang cut the traces and ran off the horses. By the time someone came along and saw the coach and passengers, the gang was long gone."

"Wouldn't there be tracks to follow?"

"No," the sheriff said, "the gang always follows the main road at least a mile or two. It's impossible to follow them."

"Then what *are* you doing?"

"Telling the judge that his niece is alive, even if she has joined the gang."

"I see," Jessie said not a little critically. "Well, now that you've done that, I suppose you will be busy trying to apprehend the Black Bandana Gang."

Malloy frowned and expelled a deep sigh. "You don't have to be so critical of me, Miss Starbuck. I'm just one man and I'm paid to protect the banks and the merchants of this town. If I go gallivantin' around the countryside, chasing shadows, and then there's a bank holdup here and people are killed, I've failed my office."

The anger went out of Jessie. "I'm sorry," she said, meaning it. "I didn't mean to be insulting. It's just that we could all see what a shock it was to the judge and his dear wife to find out that their niece was alive, but part of a gang of cutthroats."

Malloy toed the dirt. "I know Alice real well. She was one of my wife's best friends and I thought she was about as fine as a girl as I'd ever met. I can't believe this myself, but those witnesses were pretty definite."

"My hunch," Jessie said, "is that Alice was made to participate in the robbery and made to be easily identified. That would explain everything."

Malloy agreed. "I've thought of that too. I'm sure you're right. I guess this whole thing has got everyone stirred up. At least the three men that were ambushed were bachelors."

Jessie nodded, but there was small comfort to be taken in that. And Sheriff Malloy looked so dejected that she almost told him that she knew about Ferrell Taggert and that Ki was going to be going into the prison with the warden's help and the judge's blessings.

But something made Jessie withhold this information and so, without another word, she and Sheriff Malloy parted company and she went back to consult with her samurai.

★

Chapter 10

It was just past midnight and the moon above was a thin, yellow wedge as the carriage moved quietly through the low hills just east of Carson City.

After an hour Judge Davis said, "That's Warden Locke's place. His note said to just pull in behind the barn and come in the back door."

Dr. Wells nodded and turned the carriage up a long, gravel drive. The sound of the iron wheels was unnaturally loud as they crushed bits of gravel.

When they unloaded from the carriage, they moved silently to the back porch and Warden Patrick Locke was waiting with coffee.

"Find a comfortable seat," he said, leading them into a spacious living room, which was dim because Judge Davis had told the warden that he did not want anyone to know of this clandestine meeting.

"Cigar anyone?" the warden asked.

Only the judge accepted and when the warden lit the older man's cigar, Jessie took a moment to study Locke. The warden appeared to be in his mid-fifties and paunchy, but the vestiges of great physical strength could still be seen in his powerful shoulders and bull-like neck. Warden Locke was balding and he'd cut his hair very short. He wore a thin mustache but no beard and he acted like a man who was accustomed to being in charge of things.

"All right," he said, when the judge had his cigar going and everyone was sipping coffee. "What is so important that we have to meet in the middle of the night under strict secrecy?"

Jessie, Ki, and the doctor all looked to Judge Davis, because he was the man with the leverage. The judge cleared his throat and said, "This is rather unusual, Pat, but I have a special request to make of you."

The warden shifted uneasily. "I'm almost afraid to hear any more. I didn't realize that you'd bring so many friends. Who are these people?"

The judge made the introductions and ended by saying, "Miss Starbuck is, of course, the late Alex Starbuck's only child. She, like myself, was very close to Judge Archibald."

"As we all were," the warden said a little impatiently. "So what has that got to do with this meeting?"

The judge considered his cigar. "Cuban?"

"What?"

"Is this a Cuban cigar?"

"Of course!" Warden Locke snapped, "but what . . ."

"Cuban cigars are the finest in the world. I'm glad that you can afford such personal luxuries," the judge said. "Warden, what I am about to ask is, as I said, rather unusual, but . . ."

"For crying out loud!" the warden snapped. "Will you get to the point!"

Nonplussed, Judge Davis said, "The point is that I want to plant Ki in your prison so that he can learn more about the Black Bandana Gang from inmate Ferrell Taggert and whoever else he can get to talk."

"What!" Warden Locke came to his feet. "Judge, have you been drinking?"

"Of course not! Sit down, Pat!"

The warden sat but Jessie could see that he was wound as tight as a coiled spring.

Judge Davis pushed on quickly. He reminded the warden of how many people had been robbed and murdered by the gang and ended by saying, "Sheriff Malloy hasn't a clue as to who is behind all this and neither has anyone else. This county and those counties all over western Nevada are being held in a siege of terror and it won't end unless we take drastic measures."

"Judge," the warden interrupted, "I know what a strain you've been under lately. I know how much your niece means to you. But putting an innocent man into our prison would be like feeding a sheep to wolves!"

"You're wrong," Jessie said, speaking for the first time. "Ki is a samurai. He has been trained to kill, if necessary, with his bare hands. He is a warrior, Mr. Locke. To consider him a sheep is folly. He is the most dangerous man I've ever known and plenty capable of taking care of himself in any situation."

For the first time, the warden actually looked at Ki who had not said a word. The samurai was dressed in his customary black tunic and trousers.

The warden was not impressed. "He wouldn't stand a chance in my prison."

"Ki," Jessie said, "please show the warden the art of *te.*"

Dr. Wells voiced a concern. "Please, but not so vigorously that you risk opening those bullet wounds."

Ki nodded solemnly and stood up. He raised his hands and bowed to them all, then he began a routine that included all of his kicks and hand strikes. Jessie had watched the samurai do this a thousand times and knew that the performance appeared far easier than it actually was. Ki's hand and foot speed were almost unbelievable but striking at the empty air gave no indication of the samurai's power.

"Impressive, I'll admit," the warden said when the martial arts demonstration was completed, "but there are some gorillas in my prison. Men weighing nearly three hundred pounds who could rip his limbs off. Those pitty-patty little blows would not even faze my toughest inmates."

"Ki," Jessie said, "pick something and destroy it."

70

The samurai nodded. He looked around the room and then marched over to a heavy reclining chair covered with cowhide.

"Now wait just . . ."

"Haii!" the samurai shouted as he jumped up in the air and drove his right foot completely through the chair's back and retracted his foot, jumped back and allowed the iron-hard edge of his hand to crash down on the chair's heavy wooden arm.

The arm splintered into two pieces and fell to the floor.

"Jaysus!" the warden shouted. "That chair came all the way from San Francisco and cost me two hundred dollars!"

"I'll pay you for a new one," Jessie said. "What kind of wood was that arm made of?"

"Hickory from Vermont."

"It's kindling now," Jessie said. "And I wonder if you have any idea how thick that cowhide is? Why don't you take a look?"

The warden shook his head. "I don't have to look. You've made your point, Miss Starbuck. Or rather your Chinese friend has."

"I'm not Chinese," Ki said. "I'm of royal Japanese blood on my mother's side and as American as yourself on my father's side."

Jessie peeled money off a roll of one hundred-dollar bills she carried. "We apologize for ruining your favorite chair, Mr. Locke. There's enough money to buy another and an ottoman if you prefer."

"Well . . . well, thank you," the warden said. "And I stand corrected when I said your friend would be like a sheep among wolves. It appears he would be like a strange wolf among a pack of wolves. I still say it would be suicide to allow him to join those inmates."

"Ki," Jessie said, "show the warden your most unusual weapon. The one that you could sew into the lining of your prison outfit."

Ki reached into his tunic and removed a *shuriken* star blade. Both the warden and the judge looked fascinated.

71

"Select a target," Jessie said, "and demonstrate."

"Now wait a damned minute here!" the warden protested. "I don't want another . . ."

But the samurai wasn't listening and when he pointed toward a small gourd sitting atop a counter, Jessie nodded.

The samurai's hand snapped forward and the star blade flashed across the room to sever the gourd in two perfect pieces, both of which rolled off the counter to land on the floor.

The judge whistled with admiration. The warden closed his mouth and walked slowly over to dig the star blade out of his wall.

"All right," he said, "so you're a top wolf. I still say that, if they find out you've been planted to get information, you're a dead man."

"I'll take that chance."

The warden expelled a deep breath. "Judge, you sure you want to approve of this? I'm going to ask you to put it in writing so that, if anything goes wrong, it's your butt, not mine, that gets kicked."

The judge chuckled. "My butt is too old and skinny to kick anymore. Besides, what can they do to a man who is ready to retire? No," he said, "I've already taken the liberty of writing out the order and you may keep it under lock and key."

The judge reached into his coat pocket and handed the warden a letter. Locke read it quickly, nodded and placed it in his own coat pocket.

"Judge, I owe you many favors. You were the man that had the most to do with getting me my job. So I'll go along with this. And I'll even help in any way I can. But I take no responsibility."

"Agreed," Judge Davis said, puffing rapidly on the cigar.

"When?" Ki asked.

"You name the time," the warden said. "Better at night. I'll put you in isolation for a few days. That will make you look like a real hard case. When the prisoners get used to

72

having you around, I'll put you in a cell."

"The cell that Taggert is in," Jessie said.

The warden plopped down in his easy chair and blew a smoke ring up at the ceiling. "That will take some explaining," he mused. "Prisoners get pretty tight with their cell mates. We keep them four to a cell. Taggert's cell is full."

"There must be some way to get one man out," the judge said.

"Sure," the warden said. "But it'll take a little thought."

"Think about it while I'm in solitary confinement," Ki said.

Locke nodded. "I can't give you any favors, Ki. Solitary is hard time. You'll shiver all night and the food is bread and water."

"I'll survive."

"If I tried to give you an extra blanket or some meat, it would be noticed and . . ."

"I'll survive," Ki repeated. "No special favors."

"All right," Locke said. "You're asking for it. And once I get you in Taggert's cell, you're on your own. I can't protect you."

"I know that."

The warden looked around with obvious unease. "I've never done anything like this in my entire career. Isn't there some other way?"

The judge shook his head. "I've tried to think of one. There just is none, Pat. And we've got to find a way to break through this thing and start making some arrests."

"I know. I know. I heard about your niece being with those highwaymen. I can't believe it was really her, Judge."

"I think it probably was," Davis said wearily. "But that just means that they've found a way to make her do whatever they want. It makes me all the more determined to see this brought to a conclusion."

"When can I go in?" Ki said. "The sooner the better."

"How about tomorrow night? I can have you delivered by a federal marshal. By the time the inmates are awake, you'll be locked in solitary and we go from there."

73

"Sounds good," Ki said, wanting to get this affair started and then over with as soon as possible.

Warden Locke crushed his cigar and studied their faces. "Then if that's it, I bid you good luck and good night. Every day at the Nevada State Prison is a long one. Something you'll quickly discover, Mr. Ki."

Ki did not need to be told this. He was man who loved freedom and space. Living and managing to survive in a little cell for the next week or two was going to call upon all his mental and physical reserves. He believed he was equal to the challenge.

★

Chapter 11

Ki was shackled, wrist and ankles. His striped prison uniform was of poor quality, heavy, sticky, and woolen. Ki shrugged his shoulders uncomfortably and gripped the bars of the prison wagon.

"You'll get used to that uniform in a few days," Warden Locke said as they waited for the prison guards to join them. "It'll stop itching and you'll be damned grateful for it at night.

"This is the last time that we'll have a chance to speak openly, Ki. But if you sense that your life is in danger, then simply inform Guard Dave Rhine and he'll get you out fast."

"What does he look like?"

"Big redheaded kid. He looks dumb and trusting, but he's tough and smart. He's a man I can count on and so can you."

Ki nodded. "What is my crime and background?"

"You have no background. You're just a drifter who murdered a prospector about a hundred miles southeast of here near a town named Bullfrog. The prospector's body was found and the crime briefly reported in a few newspapers. The authorities believed you killed old Jed Mason for his gold."

"I see."

"Mason was a character and a loner. His gold was never found and since there were no witnesses or real evidence, you get off with a sentence of thirty years in prison. You would have hanged if the evidence would have been stronger."

"Thirty years in prison is a death sentence to some men. Do most people think that I'm supposed to have the gold squirreled away for my old age?"

"Yes," the warden said. "That's your edge. Maybe you can use the lure of gold to tempt Ferrell Taggert into a friendship. If he figures you have enough gold hidden somewhere south of here, he might even try to figure a way to spring you and himself from prison."

"Has anyone ever escaped?"

"Not since I've been warden. But you could be the first, if it served our purposes."

"I'll keep that in mind," said Ki. "Besides Guard Rhine, does anyone but yourself know my true identity?"

"No. And even Rhine has no idea why you're doing this."

"Good."

They both heard a door open and then two guards came sauntering out, each toting sawed-off shotguns. The warden stepped back and his voice assumed a rough tone when he addressed the guards.

"You men watch out for this one," he warned. "Ki is deadly."

"Is that his name?"

"Yes," the warden said. "And don't be deceived by his appearance. He might not look dangerous, but he is."

"Come on, Warden. All he did was cave in some helpless old miner's skull."

"That's right," Warden Locke said, "but he also nearly dismantled a deputy down in Bullfrog who made the mistake of stepping into his cell."

The guards looked more closely at their prisoner in the moonlight. One said, "He sure don't look that tough to me, but we'll take your word and be damned careful."

"Good," Lock said, "now get him locked up tight in solitary. A couple of days on bread and water ought to take some of the meanness out of him."

The guards chuckled and climbed up onto the wagon which had a special bench seat. One half faced forward so that the driver could see where he was heading, the other half faced backward so that the guard could watch his prisoner. There was a three-inch opening through which the guard could also empty his shotgun in case the prisoner somehow found a weapon.

"Hee-yaw!" the driver called, sending the pair of horses forward.

Warden Locke stepped back and watched as Ki passed him, hands gripping the bars, face bleak. Goodbye, he thought. I wouldn't give you the chance of a snowball in hell of getting through the next week alive.

The solitary confinement cell was six feet square, just a hole in the ground covered with an iron grate. Every quarter hour a guard would pass overhead. It was not unusual for the meaner guards to urinate down upon the prisoner just to make his existence even more miserable.

Ki *was* miserable and he was urinated upon by the guards at night when no one was watching. In the day he sat alone or exercised in the hole, practicing his *te*. The guards who watched him from above teased him cruelly.

"Hey, Sing Song Charlie!" one would call before breaking into coarse laughter. "What the hell you doing, trying to swat or kick flies outa the air!"

Ki ignored the man as he did all the others who heckled him. Even Dave Rhine, the guard that Warden had said would help him in an emergency, often taunted Ki, though he never urinated on him.

Twice, inmates passed overhead on some errand or other, and they both stared down hard at the imprisoned samurai but said nothing. Ki discovered that the warden had been correct when he'd said that the woolen prison uniform would stop itching. Also, it was pretty much a necessity to ward off the chill of the night air. It seemed that the cold dropped into the hole where Ki was huddled and left him gritting his teeth to keep them from chattering.

Bread and water was lowered down to him every morning and evening on a chain, the bread soaking in the water. The food gave the samurai no strength and by the end of three days, he felt dizzy and light-headed.

"I have to be strong," he told himself over and over.

On the morning of the fourth day, Ki looked up to see Warden Locke and two armed prison guards.

"Prisoner Ki, on your feet!" Locke commanded.

Ki stood, feeling the shackles grate at his wrists and ankles.

"Prisoner, my men will lower a ladder. You are to climb it looking neither to the left nor the right and when you are topside, you will stand at attention until orders are given. Is that clearly understood?"

"Yeah."

"You say, 'yes sir, Mr. Warden!' "

Ki looked up with insolence. "Yessir, Mr. Warden," he said in a mocking voice.

"Lower the ladder," the warden ordered.

Ki had no trouble climbing up the rickety ladder. The moment his body cleared ground level he tasted fresh air and he breathed in deeply.

"Attention, prisoner!"

The samurai climbed off the ladder and stood, but not at attention.

One of the guards kicked him behind the knees and Ki went down hard.

"Get up!" Warden Locke ordered.

Ki got up and this time he did stand at attention. Locke shouted, "You yellow-bellied sonofabitch! You killed a helpless old man for his gold and you're never going to live long enough to get out and spend it! You understand me!"

Ki said nothing.

Locke wasn't finished. "I'm going to break you in my prison. You're going to tell me where that old man's gold is hidden so it can go where it belongs—to that prospector's next of kin!"

Ki challenged Locke with his eyes and then he threw back his head and laughed.

Locke hit him in the face. It was more of a slap than a punch, but looked and sounded vicious. Ki went down.

"Get the prisoner to his feet!" Locke shouted. "And get him to cell number 7!"

Ki was yanked to his feet. Pretending to be dazed by the warden's punch, he allowed himself to be half-dragged, half-carried to cell 7.

"Prisoners stand back from the door!"

When the prisoners did as ordered, Ki's shackles were removed before the cell door was unlocked and the samurai was thrown inside. The cell was relocked and the guards moved away.

Ki shook his head and climbed unsteadily to his feet. He looked up to see three grubby prisoners staring at him without a trace of sympathy or kindness.

"Hello," Ki finally said, grabbing the bars and pulling himself erect. "My name is Ki."

"Your name is shithead, Chinaman," the largest of the three growled. "And we don't like you Oriental sonsabitches."

"That's your problem," Ki said, taking the big man's measure. "Which bunk is mine?"

"You're sleeping on the floor," the big man said.

Ki wondered if the big man was Ferrell Taggert. There were two sets of bunk beds and all but one were occupied. "I guess I'll take the empty one on top," he said to no one in particular.

The big man, who had been reclining on one of the lower bunks, rolled off of it and balled his fists. "I guess you don't understand English so well, huh Chinaman? I said, you are sleeping on the floor like a dog."

"You tell him, Niger," one of the others said. "Break his goddamn neck."

Ki stepped back against the bars and took a fighting stance. He was in poor shape. His bullet wounds were still not completely healed and he was very weak from both his convalescence and his recent diet of bread and water. Still, from the murderous expression on Niger's face, he was in for a brutal fight.

The samurai, wanting to end the fight quickly and knowing he could not match strength with the larger man, struck first. The edge of his hand smashed down hard at the base of Niger's skull and made his knees buckle. But then, the man growled and began to throw punches from all angles.

The samurai ducked and drove his stiffened fingers into the man's solar plexis and Ki watched Niger's face turn fish-white. Even so, Niger managed to grab him around the waist in a crushing bear hug.

"I'll break your fuckin' back!" he roared.

And Niger was plenty capable of doing it so Ki pulled away and stabbed the man in both eyes with his splayed fingers. The big man howled with pain and released the samurai. Ki struck the man twice more with the edge of his hand, once again to the base of the neck, and the last time to the throat. Niger toppled like a tree that had been chopped in half. When he fell, his head struck the bars of the door and he opened up a gash over his right eye that bled heavily.

Ki lowered his hands. He turned to the man who'd taunted Niger. "You want some of the same?"

The man shook his head. "My name is Ralph. I don't like pain."

"Then keep your mouth shut," Ki snapped.

Ki glanced at the third man who had to be Ferrell Taggert. Taggert was big and very ugly with black hair and a hooked nose. He had prominent ears and a scar across his forehead that made his brow look as if he were perpetually worried. The man looked to be in his mid-thirties and his eyes were cold and shifty.

80

Ki said, "Mister, are you looking for trouble?"

Taggert shook his head. "But don't push me, man. I say who lives and who dies in this cell. *I* am the law."

"Oh yeah?" Ki gestured toward Niger. "I thought he was the law."

"Nope. He just does what I say. Maybe now, you'll take his place."

"No thanks," Ki said, stepping over the injured man and then stripping Niger's belongings from the lower bunk and tossing them on the floor.

Ki said to the dazed Niger, "From now on, you're sleeping on the top and this is *my* bunk. Got that straight?"

Niger managed to nod. He touched his lacerated head and stared at his own fresh blood. "You sonofabitch," he whispered.

"Shut up," Taggert ordered before he returned his attention to Ki. "So how long are you in here?"

"Thirty years."

Taggert whistled softly. "Man, we are both in here for the rest of our lives."

Ki turned and stared out through the bars. "I can't serve that much time. I got too much waiting for me on the outside. Way too much."

"You mean that gold I heard the warden yelling at you about?"

"Maybe."

Taggert watched as Niger pulled himself up the bars and staggered over to lean against a wall just as far as he could get from Ki.

"Where you from, Chinaman?"

"I'm not a Chinaman!" Ki swore. "My mother was Japanese but my father was a white American, same as you. Call me a Chinaman again, I'll make you eat your teeth."

Taggert's black eyes showed the first signs of life but the anger in them was just a flicker and then it was gone. Hidden behind a veil. Watching him, it occurred to the samurai that this was a very, very deadly man. One who would never strike until his opponent was completely vulnerable and victory was guaranteed.

"Today is Sunday," Taggert said. "In an hour or so they'll let us out in the exercise yard."

Ki could not entirely stifle a groan as he stretched out on Niger's bunk. It was stone-hard and probably lice infested, but compared to the stinking pit that he'd just climbed out of, the bunk felt like a feather bed.

★

Chapter 12

Sheriff Pace Malloy's mind wandered as he listened to the minister's voice drone on and on during the funeral services. The wind was blowing grit across Carson City's ugly cemetery and Malloy was one of only a handful of citizens who had come to pay their final respects to the three dead stagecoach employees. But now, after standing with his head bowed for nearly forty-five minutes, he wished he'd stayed in his office.

"And so, dearly beloved," the minister said, "it is not for us worldly souls to understand why good, decent men were cut down in their prime by the Black Bandana Gang. After all, these three souls were only doing their job. It's not their fault that the law in this part of Nevada can't come up with so much as a clue as to who is behind these terrible acts."

The young sheriff's head snapped up and his eyes narrowed defensively. The Reverend Bob Platt was getting a little out of hand and starting to point fingers.

"But I will tell you, my brethren, if the law can't stop the murderin' then the citizens will rise up, and with the help of the Lord God Almighty, they will have their vengeance. And the Lord will be glad."

"Now wait just a damned minute, Bob," the sheriff snapped. "This is supposed to be a service for those dead men, not a damned platform calling for vigilante justice!"

The reverend lowered his Bible. "Sheriff Malloy, I made no such a call. I just said that, whenever in history the authorities failed to protect the people, then the people have risen up and remembered the Lord's words that 'justice be thine own'!"

"I don't remember reading that in the Bible," Malloy snapped.

"Well what about 'an eye for an eye and a tooth for a tooth'?" the reverend demanded. "Surely you remember that!"

"Well yeah, but . . ."

"Justice will be done," the reverend said, cutting Malloy off before he could form a good argument. "And personally, Sheriff, I think that the people have been patient enough already."

Sheriff Pace Malloy felt a ball of anger forming in the pit of his stomach. "Listen here now, Reverend. The surest way to get even more good people killed is to start everyone thinking that they should take the law in their own hands. Innocent blood will be shed and they'll remember that you were the cause of it."

"And I would say unto them, judge not lest ye be judged, brothers!"

To this, several of those in attendance nodded their heads in vigorous agreement causing the sheriff to snort in disgust and stomp out of the cemetery and climb onto his horse. He knew now that he could wait no longer to interrogate Ferrell Taggert. Something had to break soon in this case or there really would be a ground swell of vigilantism.

Two hours later Sheriff Malloy was sitting in the warden's office and he was angry all over again.

"I mean to see and talk to inmate Taggert," he said hotly. "All I'm asking is some professional courtesy on your part."

"And all I'm asking," Warden Locke said, also in danger of losing his temper, "is that you tell me what possible good might come of bringing inmate Taggert into this office and asking him a bunch of questions."

"I think he knows who's behind the Black Bandana Gang!" The sheriff bounced out of his chair and began to pace up and down the room. "Do you understand what I'm saying? Ferrell Taggert, in my opinion, was one of them."

"You got any proof of that?"

"No, it's just a hunch, but I'm usually right about these sorts of things."

The warden lit a Cuban cigar but did not offer one to the young sheriff. "All right, Malloy, suppose that you are right. Suppose that inmate Taggert really does know who is behind that vicious gang. Why would he tell you or me?"

"Because we both know that, if we spoke up in his behalf at the next parole board hearing, he'd stand a better than even chance of getting set free."

"He won't be eligible for parole for another three years."

"Then I'll talk to the judge," Malloy argued. "We've got to offer the man something for his information. Won't you at least give it a try? This gang is terrorizing western Nevada and we haven't been able to do a thing about it."

"That's your responsibility, not mine," Locke said in an uncompromising voice.

Sheriff Malloy threw up his hands. "Come on, Pat, what is there to lose by trying!"

The warden sighed. He was caught between the sheriff and Judge Davis, and the whole thing was complicated by having the samurai planted in Taggert's cell two weeks earlier. Still, the sheriff was right, what was there to lose?

Warden Locke came out of his seat and walked silently past the sheriff to his door. He opened the door and said to the waiting guard. "Bring inmate Taggert here at once."

"Yes sir!"

Malloy heaved a deep sigh of relief. "Thank you," he said.

Fifteen minutes later Ferrell Taggert was escorted into the warden's office by two guards. The man was shackled and when the door closed and he was alone with the sheriff and the warden, he studied them with hate-filled eyes.

"Go ahead, Sheriff," the warden said, "this is your show."

Malloy came up face to face with Taggert. The prisoner's appearance was quite unnerving because his eyes had no more humanity in them than those of a snake. But it was also that Taggert was filthy and smelled of sweat and he looked hard and desperate.

"How's it going in here?" Malloy asked quietly.

"You don't need me to tell you the answer to that one," Taggert said with a cold smile. "And I'm sure you didn't come here to make sure that I'm having fun behind bars. So cut the bullshit and say whatever you came to say."

Malloy had always appreciated directness. "All right. You know that you'd have swung by a rope if I hadn't told the judge that I thought you deserved life instead of death."

Taggert neither denied nor acknowledged this statement, but both the sheriff and the warden took this as tacit acceptance.

"So I think you owe me something and if you cooperate and tell us what you know about the Black Bandana Gang, then both the warden and I will help you get an early parole."

"Now wait just a minute!" Locke protested. "I said nothing about that."

"Yeah, but you would," the sheriff challenged. "And together, we could get you out of this hellhole the first time that you become eligible for parole."

"No big thing."

"Maybe even sooner," the sheriff added. "But this is your only chance. You got to tell us what you know right now, or it's no deal."

"How do I know you'd keep your end of the bargain?" Taggert said. "Once you got your gang, then I could rot in here for all you'd care."

"We'd put it in writing. A full letter to the parole board and we'd file it with the court so that it was on the record and couldn't be changed."

Taggert used a dirty fingernail to dig at an ingrown hair at the point of his chin. "I ain't sayin' I know anything," he finally drawled. "What I'd say was all just a suppose. Is that understood?"

The warden nodded grimly. "I'll take the notes."

Taggert frowned. "Just suppose you were a man who had been badly wronged by the courts. Maybe even by the whole law profession in Nevada."

"What are you saying?" the sheriff demanded. "You got to . . ."

"I ain't sayin' anything more than what I'm saying!" Taggert growled. "I say more, not even prison walls or iron bars could keep enemies from taking my life."

"All right," Malloy said, "go ahead."

"I'm just saying that, I suppose, that whoever is behind this whole thing might just be considered a man of some standing in the community. He might be a man with some money and a past that demands vengeance."

"Against who?" the warden asked, looking up from the pad of paper he was scribbling across.

"And," the sheriff added, "for what injustice?"

Taggert swallowed. "I just guess I've said enough."

"Come on man!" the sheriff cried. "You told us nothing!"

"I told you enough to get me killed," Taggert said. "Now what about that letter to the parole board."

"Hell no!" Malloy swore. "Not without a whole lot more specifics. And I mean names and everything."

"Uh-uh," Taggert said, wagging his head back and forth. "I ain't sayin' a damn thing more. Maybe I said too much already. And besides, you promised me a letter."

"And we'll keep our promise, but you have to tell us more."

"I can't," Taggert said, clenching his jaw with stubborn determination. "You think about what I said and see if it don't put some ideas in your head. But not a word it came from me! You say one word, and I'm a dead man."

The warden dropped his pencil on the pad of paper. He regarded his notes and shook his head. "Guards!"

The door opened and the pair of guards who'd brought Ferrell Taggert appeared. They were ordered to return the prisoner to his cell.

"No! Wait!" Taggert cried. "First, I got to look roughed up so that the prisoners will think you sent for me to be punished."

Warden Locke knew the man was right. "Go ahead," he said to the larger of the guards.

The guard yanked free a pair of leather gloves that had been tucked behind his belt. He pulled them on and said, "This is going to hurt me worse than it will hurt you."

Taggert stiffened and stared at the man with cold hatred. "You egg-suckin' whore," he hissed.

The guard cursed and his gloved fist crashed into Taggert's face smashing the inmate's lips to pulp. Taggert almost crumpled. His hands started to come up to protect his face but he found the will to pull them back down to his side.

"Your mother is a whore too," he breathed, forming little bloody bubbles.

The guard made a choking sound in his throat and hit Taggert so hard the man twisted completely around to take a tremendous uppercut in his belly. Taggert's eyes bugged and he collapsed to the floor, gasping like a beached fish.

Sheriff Malloy had to look away.

"Get him back to his cell," the warden said in a small voice. "Get him out of here right now!"

Malloy looked up to see the guards dragging the inmate out the door. "I guess," he whispered, "there won't be anyone suspicious of what we brought him in for now."

Warden Locke nodded grimly. He glanced down at the pad of paper and his sparse, scribbled notes. Not much good there, he thought.

"I could stand a drink," the warden said, "how about you?"

"Yeah," the sheriff said, defeat heavy in his voice, because, like the warden, he believed that nothing useful had been gained from this brutal encounter. "I damn sure could."

Chapter 13

When they dumped Ferrell Taggert back in his cell, even Ki was shocked by his fellow inmate's physical appearance. Taggert's lips were a bloody pulp and the man was pale and trembling.

Niger bent down and easily picked Taggert up, then placed him on his lower bunk. "Them sonofabitches really worked you over, huh. What'd they want?"

"They'd heard rumors we were plannin' a breakout next month," Taggert said through clenched teeth. "I told 'em it wasn't true. They didn't believe me."

"Bastards!" the third man in their cell, whose name was Carl Pinkton, swore. Pinkton was a rapist and the only words he uttered were obscenities.

"Give me a drink," Taggert groaned.

Niger found a chipped enamel cup and gave Taggert a drink. The inmate swirled the water around in his mouth, then spat it on the floor of the cell.

"Just let me sleep awhile," Taggert said.

Two days later Taggert's lips were still caked with blood and puffy when he pulled the samurai aside in the court-yard.

"Listen," Taggert said in a quiet voice meant for Ki's ears

alone. "I've been thinking a lot about you and me for the last couple of days."

"Why?"

"We need to get out of here. We won't last thirty years behind these rock walls. And even if we did, we'd be old men when we got out."

Ki said nothing.

"How much gold," Taggert said, eyeing the samurai closely, "did you get from that prospector you killed down around Bullfrog?"

It was not an unexpected question. In fact, Ki had been waiting for Taggert to ask it right from the beginning. Now, the trick was to sound cagey and convincing.

"Why do you ask?"

"I'm askin'," Taggert said, "because if you can pay the price, I think I can find men that will help us break outa this shithole prison. But it'll be risky and no one is going to do it cheap. So can you afford it, or not!"

"How much?"

"Ten thousand, minimum."

Ki sucked in a deep breath and expelled it slowly. "That's a lot of money," he said. "It wouldn't leave me any fortune."

"Man," Taggert hissed, "how much fun can you have spending the next thirty years of your life in this place!"

Ki was silent for a moment. "How do I know you aren't just setting me up?"

"Simple," Taggert said, "I plan it and we go out together. Then we ride down to Bullfrog and dig up that buried treasure of yours and you pay us off."

Ki nodded. "Ten thousand in gold, huh?"

"It's a bargain against thirty years of our lives."

"Why do I need you?" Ki asked bluntly.

"Because I got the connections, goddammit!" Taggert leaned closer. "You ever hear of the Black Bandana Gang?"

"Sure. Who hasn't?"

"Well I rode with them. The brains of it ain't afraid to try anything if the price is right—and ten thousand dollars would be enough."

"Maybe I need to think about it," Ki hedged, not wanting to sound too eager.

"Think about it! Jeezus, Ki! What's to think about? We either rot in this place or we buy ourselves freedom! Man, there's nothing at all to think about."

Ki's brow furrowed deeply as he pretended to ponder the proposition. He waited until Ferrell Taggert looked as if he were ready to explode, then he said, "All right, ten thousand."

"Good!" Taggert smiled for the first time since Ki had laid eyes on the man. "I'll get the word out."

"Ten thousand, then," Ki said.

"He may want a few thousand more. Can you do it?"

Ki swore softly. "Yeah," he finally said. "If I had to."

"That's my man!" Taggert said with a wide grin. "I'll bet you've got twice, maybe three times that much buried out there someplace. Right?"

In answer, the samurai grinned tightly.

"You sly sonofabitch!" Taggert said, almost to the point of laughter. "You and me are going to have a high old time together after we get free of this place. I know some wild, wild women that will make you think that you're wallowing around in paradise."

Ki chuckled. "I can hardly wait to see them."

"Oh, you will, man! 'Course, like the man that will figure a way to get us out of here, those kind of women don't do anything for free."

"Don't worry about it," Ki said. "I got enough gold to make 'em do anything we want, whenever we want."

Ferrell Taggert licked his lips. "I knew when you whipped Niger that there was something special about you, man. I knew right then. You and me, we're going to have some good times together before we are through."

"Yeah," Ki said.

"But don't say a word of this to anyone. Not to Pinkton, and especially not to Niger. They'd just want to be a part of it and it would make things that much harder for the boss to figure out."

91

"Mind telling me who he is?" Ki asked, trying to sound disinterested.

"Hell, yes, I mind!" Taggert lowered his voice. "Listen, only a couple of people like myself know who's behind the Black Bandana Gang. And if they ever talk, their lives wouldn't be worth spit. So I ain't talking."

"But what if this man decides not to help us?"

Taggert was slow to answer. Finally, however, he said, "If he won't help us, then maybe I will talk. That's what that thing was the other day, you know."

"You mean when you were beat up?"

"Sure! Sheriff Malloy was trying to jerk me over to his side. He said, if I told him who was behind the gang, he'd try to get me paroled. But man, I won't even be eligible for three more years! There's no way I want to stay in this hell that long. That's why I told him and the warden to shove it up their ass."

Taggert leaned closer. "If the Boss Man decides to accept our ten-thousand-dollar offer, we'll be out of here in less than a week."

"You really think he could do that?"

"Yeah," Taggert said. "He knows who to bribe in this place and he has the money and the people to do it."

"I hope I get a chance to meet him," Ki said.

"Oh, don't worry. If he takes our offer, he'll be wanting to come down to Bullfrog just to protect his investment. That much I can guarantee."

"Does he live close?"

"Close enough," Taggert said, his eyes narrowing. "But don't you worry none about him. You just worry about finding that cache of gold that you took from the prospector you killed."

Taggert swallowed nervously. "Let me tell you something, Ki. If you couldn't find the gold or something happened that you couldn't pay the Boss Man off, then we'd both be strung up from a tree and have pieces of our hides stripped away until we went mad with pain and the Boss Man cut our balls off and let us bleed to death."

"This man sounds like he means business."

"Hell, yes, he does!" Taggert lowered his voice. "Just don't plan on crossing him whatever you do. It'd be a fatal mistake for both of us."

"No double cross," the samurai vowed.

Ferrell Taggert's black and bloated lips formed the semblance of a smile and then, as a prison guard blew a sharp whistle signaling that the exercise period was over, Taggert moved away.

★

Chapter 14

In a steep-sided box canyon only miles southeast of Virginia City, a tall, broad-shouldered young man stepped out of a huge tin building that housed the expensive steam equipment of the Comstock Mining Company. It was sundown and the canyon was in shadow but to the west the clouds were edged in crimson and gold.

The man was dressed in an expensive suit perfectly tailored to his manly physique, but when he slapped at his trousers he raised clouds of dust. The man was bareheaded, dark complected, and very handsome. When he saw a lovely young woman emerge from a nearby cabin and move toward him, he smiled.

"Ah, Alice," he said with a grin, as he walked toward her. "You always appear so beautiful after a hard day in the mines."

"Hard day," she said, her voice teasing. "Since when have you ever spent a hard day in your life?"

He chuckled and enfolded the woman in his arms, then kissed her passionately, unconcerned about who might see them.

When Alice Reynolds broke from his embrace, her heart was already pounding. "Allen, did you find anything promising today?"

"No." The man glanced back at the mine. "But we will. Perhaps another week, maybe two. It won't be long."

"That's what you've been saying for over a month."

The man's smile died and he listened to the sound of the giant steam engine as it lowered a fresh crew of miners six hundred feet down a steep, vertical shaft.

"I can't predict anything," the man said. "I am a geologist but if I could find gold or silver that easily, we would all be rich, and that is not the case."

"I know," Alice said, "it's just that I can't wait to be free of this place. And once we've struck it rich, he'll let us go free."

The man nodded, but he did not believe they would ever be free. "What have you cooked us for dinner tonight?"

"Chicken," Alice said. "But I'm running late. It might be another hour before we eat."

The tall, young geologist felt his eyes being pulled up toward the rims of the box canyon, and though he did not see the rifle guards, he knew that they were watching. They were always watching. No one moved a step in this place without being observed by the guards.

"Let's go inside," Allen said. "Have you a bath waiting?"

Alice nodded. "I even boiled some water so that you won't complain so bitterly this time."

Allen chuckled and slipped his arm around the young woman's slender waist. "Come on," he said, wanting to get inside where they could not be seen.

Their cabin was no larger or smaller than the other half dozen that had been hastily built in the box canyon. Inside the thirty-foot-square log structure were a few pieces of rough furniture. The floor was wood but uneven and there was a barrel stove in one corner and a huge dented tin basin in the other corner. The basin was part of a boiler that had been used in a nearby mining operation but now served very well as a bathtub.

"You feel so cold," Alice said as they entered the cabin. "You always feel cold after working down there."

"It is cold," he said, going over to the tub and putting his finger in to test the water. "Ahhh, but this will warm me up in a hurry."

The man undressed quickly, giving his clothes to the young woman, who set his starched shirt and underclothes aside to be washed early the following morning. His coat and pants would simply be shaken free of their dust and his black shoes did not yet need polishing.

Allen stepped into the basin and then he sighed happily as he lowered himself into the water.

"It feels wonderful," he told her. "You should come in and join me."

Her eyebrows raised in question. "If I did that, now how would the chicken get cooked and dinner be served?"

Allen shrugged. "Pour another kettle of hot water in and join me. The dinner can wait."

"Are you sure?"

"Of course," he said, feeling desire cause his manhood to lift under the water. "But lock the door first."

Alice locked the cabin door by dragging their bed over a few feet. Then she slipped out of her dress and underclothes and pirouetted before him.

"Come on," he said with more than a little urgency. "Quit showing it off."

"And why shouldn't I 'show it off'?" she asked, her voice faintly pouting.

"No reason at all," he said, feeling his mouth go dry as she moved seductively across the room toward him.

When she climbed into the tub, Allen did not scoot over but instead, reached out and spread her thighs wide apart.

"Sit," he ordered.

Alice put one hand on his shoulder and used the other to grab his already stiff rod. Looking deep into his eyes, she licked her lips and slowly slid down, wetly impaling herself.

"Ohhh, Allen," she moaned, wiggling her bottom as she felt him rise up deep inside of her. "I was hoping you'd ask me to share this with you again tonight."

96

He leaned forward and his tongue flicked at her hard nipples causing her to gasp with pleasure. "Don't I ask you every day after work?"

"Yes, and I guess that's why we always eat so late," she said, slowly raising herself only to slide down his rod again, experiencing a pleasure so exquisite that it made her toes tingle.

Allen began to suck on her right breast and she whimpered softly, her hips moving a little faster. After several minutes, he sucked on the other breast until her body was moving rapidly up and down on his thick root.

"I'm dirty," he panted, "you should wash me."

She pushed back from him and tried to still her body. Alice's eyes were glazed with pleasure and she seemed not to understand what he was saying.

"Here," he said, reaching over the side of the tub and grabbing a bar of soap and a washrag, "wash my back, please."

Alice soaped up the washrag and made an honest attempt to scrub his muscular back when he leaned forward, but when he began to pay attention to her breasts she could do nothing except move faster and faster on his thick rod.

"I can't," she panted. "Please, later."

"All right," he said, leaning back against the side of the basin, laughter in his eyes. "Have your way with me, then."

Alice moaned and closed her eyes. He watched as she bit her lower lip and he liked the way her breasts bounced as she lost control of her body.

A few minutes later, she cried out and began to bounce wildly up and down. Allen smiled as he laced his hands behind his head and gave her everything that she wanted and more.

Late that night, Allen left her sleeping soundly. He dressed in darkness and slipped out of their cabin to move silently across the mining compound toward a cabin that was slightly larger than the others.

"Who goes there!" a guard challenged in the dark.

"It's me, Allen!" he answered with annoyance.

"Oh, sorry. But the Boss Man says you're supposed to call out before you get within . . ."

"I know, I know. I just forgot."

"Forgettin'," the guard said, "could get you shot. I got my orders, you know, same as everyone else."

Allen had no patience with the man and moved on by. He entered the log cabin and stood, allowing his eyes to adjust to the light.

"You're late," the man said. "I don't like that."

"I'm sorry," Allen apologized. "I worked late and by the time we got finished with dinner, it was almost eleven. Then I had to give Alice time to fall asleep and . . ."

"Sit down."

Allen sat. As always, the Boss Man was wearing his black bandana. Allen had never seen his face and he never expected to.

"What's up?"

The Boss Man studied him in silence. "I'm not sure," he said when Allen finally started to squirm a little. "But I want you to ask the girl about her uncle, Judge Davis. There seems to be something going on between him and the warden and a rich woman named Jessica Starbuck."

"I've even heard of her—or at least her family name."

"Who hasn't," the man said cryptically. "Just find the connection between the three of them."

"Alice might not know of any connection."

"Ask, or I'll take her along on another job."

Allen shook his head. "I don't think she could take another one. Not even if you swear to kill her uncle—or me."

The man laughed, but it was an ugly sound. "You've told me she's your love slave. That she can't get enough of you."

Allen said, "She . . . she loves me. She has no idea that I came into this voluntarily. She thinks we'll escape together soon."

"I don't care what she thinks. All I care about is making this mine pay off. How much longer?"

98

Allen's mouth went dry. "I think it's going to take a few more weeks to strike ore."

The Boss Man's fist slammed down on the table between them with such force that a full bottle of whiskey jumped up and spilled its contents.

"Do you know how much money I've put into that hole in the ground you promised me was a sure winner!"

Allen shrank back, feeling the whiskey leak onto his pants and not daring to even move. "I swear that the Comstock Lode runs directly under this canyon. It's just a matter of getting down there deep enough to tap into it!"

Boss Man leaned forward. His voice cut at the geologist when he hissed, "You've got the girl for another two weeks. If you don't strike a vein by then, I'll find another use for her."

"No, please!"

"Two weeks," the man said, "and you'd better bring me some pay dirt or I'll use your pretty little lovebird for my own pleasure!"

Allen's chin dipped up and down rapidly. "Yes sir," he vowed. "Two weeks."

"Get out of here!" Boss Man snarled. "If you spent more energy in our shaft instead of using your own shaft on that girl, maybe we'd already have gold."

"No sir," he breathed, scrambling up from his chair and hurrying out the door.

"Allen!"

He froze.

"Is she good?" Boss Man purred. "Is she as good as she looks?"

He swallowed and his voice was as dry as the desert sand. "She's not, I swear it. She don't know much about pleasuring a man. Not much at all."

"We'll see," Boss Man chuckled. "If you don't strike ore for me in two weeks, we'll just see."

Allen felt sweat bead across his forehead as he flung open the cabin door and plunged outside, gasping for fresh Comstock air.

★

Chapter 15

Jessie and Dr. Wells had been running around in circles ever since their arrival in Carson City. They had tracked down one dead-end clue after another and, like Sheriff Malloy, were nearly at their wits' end.

"It looks like our best and really only hope is that Ki will be able to find out something in prison," Jessie said with resignation.

The doctor nodded. During the past few days he had been assisting old Doc Wallace, one of Carson City's first medical practioners, in his office.

"At least I'm doing something of consequence," he said. "Yesterday I helped Dr. Wallace make a very difficult delivery. I think the baby would have died if I hadn't been there."

"I'm glad," Jessie told him. "Tonight, we're supposed to be paid a visit by Warden Locke. I'm getting pretty anxious about Ki. It's been what, three weeks now?"

"Almost," the doctor said. "I guess he couldn't find a way to escape and we'll have to pull him out of there."

"Oh," Jessie said, "he could escape if he wanted. My guess is that he just hasn't found out enough information from Taggert yet. But when he does, we'll hear from him. Hopefully, the warden will have something important to tell us tonight."

"What about the sheriff?" Dr. Wells asked. "Is he still dogging your heels?"

"He knows that I'm up to something," Jessie said. "I think he's an honest lawman, but he sure can't stand the idea that someone might steal his thunder."

"You'd think that he'd appreciate all the help he could get on this one. Especially considering that the Black Bandana Gang just robbed a bank in Gold Hill and shot down three men. Sheriff Malloy ought to be thinking that it could just as well have happened in this town."

Jessie agreed, and for the rest of the afternoon and evening she could scarcely rest or enjoy a meal.

It was nearly eleven o'clock at night when a soft knock sounded on Jessie's door.

"Who is it?"

"Warden Locke."

Jessie recognized the man's voice and unlocked the door. The warden, looking harried and fretful, hurried inside, closing and locking the door on his own.

"I have news," he said. "Do you have any whiskey or something to drink?"

Jessie nodded and went to a cabinet where she produced a bottle of brandy and another of rye.

"I'd prefer the brandy."

She poured him a stiff drink, then one for herself and realized that there was a tremor in her hand. It was Ki. Jessie was desperately worried that the samurai's true purpose might be uncovered and he came to harm in that horrible prison.

"All right," she said when the warden had taken his drink. "What have you heard?"

"Ki has gained the confidence of Taggert. The man really believed our story about Ki killing a prospector down south and burying his gold. For the promise of ten thousand dollars of Ki's buried gold, supposed members of the Black Bandana Gang are going to attempt to spring them from prison."

"When!"

"In a few days." The warden shrugged. "I wish I could be more specific, but the message that I received from Ki through Dave Rhine was quite brief. Ki just let us know that a breakout was planned and that we should let it happen and not risk lives interfering."

"How are you going to do that?" Jessie asked.

"I'm really not sure. Of course, I can't tell my guards to step aside. Not unless I explain everything to them and that would risk a leak that could jeopardize Ki's life."

"No," Jessie agreed. "You can't do that."

"So we'll just have to wait and hope that the escape goes smoothly and that none of my guards are killed."

"I know that Ki will do everything in his power to prevent that from happening," Jessie said.

"Sure," the warden answered, "but the question is—given the circumstances he's caught up in—will he have any control over things during the breakout?"

"Ki always has control," Jessie said. "And whenever the breakout happens, I promise you, he will be in charge even if Taggert and his henchmen aren't aware of the fact."

"I hope to hell you're right about that," the warden said, tossing down the rest of his brandy. "I want to see the Black Bandana Gang captured as well as anyone. Still, I have a responsibility to Dave Rhine and the rest of my guards. I don't like the idea of them not knowing that trouble is coming."

Jessie understood completely. "Waiting is the hardest thing in the world. But in this case I don't think we have any choice at all."

The warden helped himself to the brandy and poured another drink. "Let's suppose that Ki is able to prevent any of my guards from being killed. So what happens then? I think we can assume that whoever is in charge of the Black Bandana Gang will not be foolish enough to participate in the prison break. So I still don't see where this is heading."

"Our hope is that Ki would be taken to the man in charge,"

Jessie said, "or at least taken to his hiding place. After that, it's up to Ki."

"You're putting a hell of a lot of trust in that man," the warden said.

"He's earned it."

The warden tossed down the second drink. "I'm sure he has. But I won't sleep well until this whole thing is over and I've lost no guards. If one was killed, knowing what I know now, I'd never be able to forgive myself."

"I know," Jessie said, "I won't either."

Warden Locke left them a few minutes later.

"He's under tremendous pressure," Dr. Wells said.

"He'll hold up," Jessie said, "and in a few days, we'll finally have some answers."

The very next day as Ki was moving out to the exercise yard, Ferrell Taggert edged up beside him. "You ready to fly," the inmate whispered.

"When, tonight?"

"How about in the next five minutes?"

Ki's jaw almost dropped to his chin. "You mean in broad daylight?"

"Sure," Taggert said, his face alive with excitement. "No one has ever tried to escape in the daytime and that's when they'll least expect it."

Ki glanced up at the four guard towers atop the high, rock walls. "How are we supposed to do it?"

"Just stick close beside me, brother. In a few minutes you're going to see something not soon to be forgotten."

The samurai tensed. When Taggert moved off a ways, Ki stuck to the man like his shadow. Taggert moved over to the front wall and they watched as the gate was opened the daily supply wagon used to bring back food and laundry rolled into the compound under heavy guard and was inspected in preparation to leaving.

"All right," Taggert whispered, "get ready."

"For what? I . . ."

Suddenly, a stick of dynamite came spinning over the wall

and it must have had a short fuse because it exploded almost on impact right below the gate. The impact was so powerful that it rocked the nearest guard tower and before the guards could recover, more sticks of dynamite were spinning over the walls and exploding. One landed on the administrative office and blew its roof to kindling. The office's heavy door was thrown seventy or eighty feet into the air.

Ki heard gunfire and shouting, which was instantly smothered by a tremendous explosion that actually knocked a hole through the thick rock wall. A horde of screaming prisoners rushed the hole, bent on escape.

Smoke and dust blanketed the compound and Ki barely could see the guards as they opened fire on the mob of howling inmates desperately trying to escape. The samurai saw prisoners go down under the gunfire, and yet a few did reach the hole in the wall and vanish.

"Come on!" Taggert shouted over the din and confusion as he raced for the supply wagon and threw himself inside.

Ki dove in beside him hearing more dynamite exploding. It sounded like a full-scale war was underway.

"Get in that empty flour barrel!" Taggert shouted.

Ki did as he was told and Taggert slammed the lid down tight. Ki could hear the sound of muffled gunfire but no more explosions. Locked in a bent position, muscles cramping, it seemed to take hours before he heard a guard shout and the supply wagon lurched forward.

When the wagon did not stop, Ki knew that they had to be leaving the prison.

"They did it," Ki whispered to himself as his muscles cramped and he felt as if he would suffocate if he did not soon have fresh air.

An eternity later, the wagon stopped and the top was ripped from the barrel.

"Outa there!" a man cried.

Ki could not move because there was no circulation in his limbs. The man swore and knocked the barrel open spilling the samurai across the bed of the supply wagon.

"Help him, gawdamn you!" someone else yelled. "Get them both mounted and get that wagon on down the road before someone comes along!"

Ki and Taggert were dragged out of the supply wagon and tossed onto the back of a horse. The pain in the samurai's legs was excruciating.

"I told you they'd do it, didn't I?" Taggert gritted through his teeth.

The sun was blinding and before Ki's eyes could adjust to the sudden brightness, the horse he was riding was whipped into a run. It was all the samurai could do to keep his seat.

"Yahoo!" Taggert screamed hoarsely. "We're free!"

Ki gripped the saddlehorn and tried to hang on with his thighs until he got some circulation back into the lower part of his legs and his bare feet.

He squinted into the sun and through the flying dust and grit, he judged that there were no less than ten mounted riders surrounding him, and every damn one of them was wearing a black bandana.

The samurai risked a glance back over his shoulder. He could hear the fading sounds of heavy gunfire and see black smoke roiling up from the prison. He wondered how many inmates had been cut down in the foolish try for escape under the guards' rifles.

Ten? Twenty? It obviously did not matter to Taggert and the men that surrounded him. And Ki knew without question that, once these men realized that he did not have a treasure of gold buried in some town called Bullfrog, his own life wasn't going to be worth spit.

★
Chapter 16

Ki had been blindfolded as soon as his daring liberators had put a few miles between themselves and the Nevada State Prison. For two more hours, they had ridden through rough hill country without any conversation. And now they had finally come to a halt.

"How about letting me take this damn thing off?" he asked.

"Not yet." Ki recognized Taggert's voice. "Dismount and don't say anything until you're asked to."

Ki did as he was told. Someone jerked his arms behind his back and tied his wrists.

"What the hell is this for?"

"Just shut up and you'll be fine," a rough voice said.

Ki was shoved into a room and then made to sit on a rickety chair.

"Leave us alone," a voice commanded.

Ki heard a door close, and then the commanding voice said, "So, you owe us ten thousand dollars in gold."

"Not until I'm free and this isn't free."

The voice hardened. "Why don't you tell me where the gold is hidden so I can send a few of my men after it. Once we have it, we can take our ten thousand and you can have your freedom and the rest."

Ki laughed. "You must think I'm awfully stupid."

"Then am I to understand that you are refusing to cooperate?"

The question was asked very softly, but nothing could veil the hard malice it contained. Despite himself, the samurai felt a shiver of dread pass through his body.

"I'll cooperate," he said, "but on my own terms."

Ki was not prepared for the swiftness of the blow that struck him flush on the jaw and sent him crashing over backward to sprawl across the floor. He tried to spring to his feet, but with his wrists bound behind him and blinded by the bandana he was helpless.

A terrible pain exploded against his left side and the samurai groaned and tried to roll away from the man who was putting the boot to him. He was not successful and another kick folded him up like a wet newspaper and left him struggling to retain consciousness.

"*Your* terms?" the voice mocked. "Is that what I heard you say?"

Ki was sure that the man would break every bone in his body if he didn't do his will. "All right," he wheezed, "but I have to go and find that buried gold myself. It isn't marked and your men would never find it on their own."

Powerful hands clenched onto the samurai's throat and cut off his air supply. Ki struggled, caught like a rabbit in a trap, and for a moment he finally did lose consciousness. The hands, however, loosened their hold and Ki was jerked back up into the wooden chair.

"If you're playing games with me, I'll see that you are staked out in Death Valley and I'll personally watch you cook to death. You ever see a man die of thirst?"

Ki shook his head.

"It's a terrible way to die. It'll take about two days down there and you'll scream as if your eyes were being pecked out by crows."

Ki managed to shake his head. "I didn't go to prison for nothing," he choked. "I killed that prospector and buried his gold where no one could find it."

107

There was a long silence during which the samurai's heart pounded wildly in his ears.

"All right," the voice finally decreed. "You will leave within the hour. Ferrell will go along with a few others. He'll know what to do if you don't come up with that buried gold."

Ki managed to nod his head. He felt sick and dizzy from the punishment he'd just taken. "Do I have to keep wearing this blindfold?"

"Yes," the man growled. "At least until you're a day's ride from here."

Ki desperately tried to think of some way to gain vital information on this man and where he was being held. "Who are you?" he blurted.

"I'm the Boss Man. I'm the one that decides who lives and who dies in this part of the country. That's all you need to know."

The man's boots sounded on the floor and then Ki was dragged to his feet and hauled outside.

"Feed him and then hit the trail south."

Taggert said, "I've been to Bullfrog. We should be there in two or three days and back in less than a week."

Boss Man said, "You know that the West isn't big enough for you if I'm double-crossed, don't you, Ferrell?"

"Yes sir!"

From the tone of Ferrell Taggert's voice, Ki could tell that he was scared.

"Good," Boss Man said. "You got one week. Now send word to Allen that I want to see him, right now."

"Sure," Taggert said quickly.

Ki was roughly hustled away. His wrists were untied and a plate of cold beans and sourdough bread was shoved into his hands. A glimmer of hope flared in the samurai's heart. With his hands free, perhaps he could pull the bandana down for a few unguarded moments. If he just catch of glimpse of a familiar mountaintop, he could determine his general location and lead a posse back to this place.

"I need something to wash it down with," he said, staring

108

up blindly and hoping his guard would have to turn away so that he could take a quick peek around.

But almost instantly, a cup of cold coffee was pushed into the samurai's hands. "You got fair warning, mister. If you reach up and touch that bandana, even to scratch, I've got orders to blow your brains all over the side of the cabin."

Ki managed to nod his head. Hope withered like a frozen flower in his heart and he told himself to be patient. That he'd have his chance to learn what he needed to know in order to break this vicious gang and kill its ruthless leader.

Patience. It was a virtue that few white men ever bothered to develop. Indians had the wisdom to cultivate patience, and that's why they were such deadly fighters, especially the Apache who were known to wait motionless for hours in the blazing sun, only to strike and kill when least expected.

"So," Allen said, pausing beside the samurai on the way to Boss Man's cabin, "you're the ten-thousand-dollar prisoner."

Ki automatically looked up toward the man who was standing before him but said nothing. And after a moment, Allen passed by and entered the Boss Man's cabin.

"Sit down."

Allen sat.

"Whiskey?"

"No thanks."

"I want you to go with Taggert and make sure that they return with that gold."

Allen took a deep breath. "Why me? There are plenty of others. Besides, I'm needed in your mine."

"You're needed," Boss Man hissed, "wherever I say you're needed."

Allen licked his lips. He knew better than to argue. "All right. But I'm taking Alice. She won't stay without me."

"She'll stay." The Boss Man chuckled. "I'll keep a close eye on her."

Allen jumped to his feet. "No, goddammit! The only reason she went on that holdup was because you convinced

109

her that you'd kill me if she refused."

"And I would have."

Allen clenched his jaw. "No, you wouldn't have. You need me too much. Without me, that mine won't produce a cent and you'll have wasted everything. And I won't go without my woman."

The Boss Man came slowly to his feet and Allen was more scared than he'd ever been before in his life. His fear increased tenfold when the Boss Man drew his sixgun, cocked it, and pointed at his face.

"You want to change your mind about the girl, or do you want to die right now?"

His throat constricted with fear. Sweat like blood ran from every pore of his body but Allen knew in his heart that he was too valuable to lose. After the mine started producing, he might be expendable, but not until then.

"Miss Reynolds goes with me or I don't go," Allen heard himself whisper in a voice that did not sound as if it belonged to him.

For a moment Allen could actually see the Boss Man tighten his grip on the trigger. He closed his eyes, unable to watch anymore while his mind screamed somewhere deep inside that he was a fool who'd signed his own death warrant.

But no shot came. No blinding flash to signal the very instant of his death. Bathed in a sweat of fear, Allen opened his eyes and saw that the Boss Man had holstered his sixgun.

"You ever defy me again, I'll see that you go screaming all the way to hell."

Allen managed to nod his head. He started to turn on legs gone wooden with fear.

"You get that gold and be back in a week or less. If the girl can't keep up, then you'll kill her! You understand me!"

"Yes sir."

"I don't trust that Chinaman. I don't trust him one damn bit. You watch him every minute or he'll up and run away. He runs away before we get that gold, it's your neck as well as Taggert's. You understand me?"

"Yes sir."

"Allen?"

Something in the Boss Man's voice made him turn around. "Sir?"

"I'll have that girl yet," Boss Man vowed. "I'll fill her with my seed before this is over."

Allen nodded his head, fear and hate washing over him in waves. Then, before he said something that would insure his death, he turned and hurried away to tell Alice that they were going on a long, hard ride south.

★

Chapter 17

Judge Davis rushed into the hotel dining room where Jessie and the doctor were having their usual noontime meal. "Miss Starbuck!" he called, causing all the other diners to gape and stop their pleasant afternoon conversations. "Dr. Wells!"

"My heavens, Judge!" Jessie exclaimed, coming to her feet when she saw Judge Davis's shocked expression. "What's wrong!"

The judge was badly winded but even so managed to blurt, "There's been a major riot and breakout this morning at the prison. I don't know much more than that except that at least a half dozen prisoners have escaped and maybe that many more have been shot down by the guards."

"What about Ki?" Jessie asked.

"I just don't know yet," the judge said. "But I've got a carriage outside and I'm on my way out there now. I was sure that you'd want to come along."

"Damn right," Dr. Wells said. "My medical kit is upstairs in my room. I'm going to need it."

"We'll be waiting in the carriage," Jessie said, hurrying after the puffing Judge.

"It sounds very bad," the judge said. "I just received word of it and came right over here before I drove out."

"I'm glad you did," Jessie said. "I pray that Ki wasn't hurt."

"It's too early to tell. But we should know about him shortly."

The doctor hurriedly rejoined them only a few moments later, and Judge Davis did not spare the whip as he sent the carriage horses racing out toward the east of town where the Carson River and the State Prison were located.

"Look!" Jessie cried, pointing to the plume of smoke rising from within the prison's walls.

They heard the occasional pop-popping sounds of distant rifle fire. Jessie clung to the doctor's arm. "When you go in there, the first thing you look for is Ki," she said.

Dr. Wells nodded grimly.

They arrived at the prison gate fifteen minutes later to see guards swarming all over the place. They noted the hole in the prison's outside wall and how one of the guard towers appeared to be in danger of collapse.

"It looks like they were attacked by an army!" Judge Davis said.

"Hold up there!" a guard shouted, jumping into their path. "This compound is sealed and . . ."

"I'm Judge Davis, you idiot! I have the authority to come and go in this place any time I wish. Now step aside."

"No, sir! Who's the other two with you, Judge?"

"Dr. Wells. I assume you've got men in need of medical attention?"

"Yes, sir. The doctor can go inside, but not the lady. Not here, Judge."

"He's right," the judge said. "Jessica, I'm afraid that they've already had one riot. Your presence might very well incite another."

"But dammit!"

"I'm sorry," the judge said. "It's for your good as well as everyone else's that you stay outside."

Jessie knew that the judge was right, but that didn't make accepting the decision any easier.

"Just find out if Ki is safe," she whispered.

113

Both the judge and the doctor nodded vigorously as Jessie disembarked from the carriage to wait anxiously outside the prison walls.

It turned out to be a very long wait. Almost two hours. When the judge finally drove his carriage back out, he looked shaken. Jessie rushed up to him. "Well?"

"Ki is gone. So is Ferrell Taggert. No one knows if they are among the prisoners who ran through the wall or not. If they were, they are probably running with the pack along the Carson River. Warden Locke has ordered men and bloodhounds to track them down. They're forming up inside the prison walls right now."

Jessie breathed a sigh of relief. Ki was alive. And she was sure that he would not run with the pack along the river but strike out with Ferrell Taggert for the Black Bandana Gang's secret hideout.

"I think he might have done it," she whispered.

"Yes," the judge said, "but at what cost? You should see the carnage inside those walls, Jessica. There are at least two guards dead and I lost count of how many prisoners were killed and wounded. The cost was too high."

Jessie nodded with grim agreement.

"I should never have allowed Ki to go in there," the judge said.

"You had no idea that it would turn out to be like this."

"I should have guessed."

"How could you?" Jessie demanded. "Who would ever have imagined that the gang would attempt a daylight escape and that they'd use sticks of dynamite to blow up the prison compound? No, Judge, this is far worse than any of us could have believed."

Davis nodded. "Your young doctor friend said that he'd be tied up for at least the next twenty-four hours. Men are dying in there and he's working fiendishly to save as many as possible."

"Take me back to town," Jessie said quietly.

The judge gave her his hand and helped Jessie up into his

114

carriage. He drove back to Carson City very slowly, his face reflecting his deep sadness over what he had just witnessed within the bloody confines of the Nevada State Prison.

"Thanks, Judge," Jessie said when he left her at her hotel.

"You should just rest," the judge said. "Just lie down and rest. There's nothing we can do now but wait to hear if they apprehend Ki along with the others."

"Sure," Jessie said. "And, Judge, I'm sorry the way this turned out. It wasn't your fault, or the warden's, or anyone else's. No one made those prisoners commit the crimes that put them behind bars and then sent them into a frenzy this morning as they attacked the guards and tried to break out."

"Yeah, I know that. But there are a lot of men that have everything to gain and nothing to lose by attempting an escape. I don't see how we could have expected them to behave otherwise."

"Judge," she told him just before he left, "we did what we thought was best. All of us. We have to stop that gang."

"Sure, but . . ."

"Go lie down," Jessie said, thinking that he looked very bad. "Have a drink or two and try to sleep. You'll see things clearer when you've calmed down."

"I hope so," he told her just before he drove away.

Jessie hurried into the hotel and up to her room. She changed from her city dress into her tight-fitting riding pants and a man's shirt.

Jessie packed her saddlebags and made sure that her sixgun as well as her derringer were loaded. And finally, she yanked her Stetson hat down to the tops of her ears, picked up her Winchester rifle, and headed for the door.

She would rent or buy a horse and saddle and chase after the warden and his bloodhounds. There would be no waiting for the news this time.

At the hotel desk, the clerk scarcely recognized her until she said, "I'll be checking out now. You can bill Starbuck Enterprises in San Francisco."

"But . . ."

"I've already okayed it with your manager," Jessie said, striding out the door.

Jessie hurried down Carson City's boardwalk. It seemed perfectly obvious to her that, if Ki was not found along the Carson River, then he had been successful in convincing Taggert about the hidden gold in Bullfrog.

Jessie had never been to Bullfrog. She had no idea where it was or how long it might take her to reach such a desolate place. All she knew for sure was that Bullfrog was where the Black Bandana Gang would take Ki.

And just as sunrise promised another sundown, she meant to be waiting in Bullfrog.

It was her only hope of saving Ki's life.

Jessie bought a fine dapple-gray mare with long legs and a deep chest that promised endurance. Galloping out of Carson City, she reached the prison only to discover that Warden Locke and a half dozen guards had already ridden off after the bloodhounds.

"You'd sure better not go out there," the guard warned.

"Thanks for the advice," Jessie said, ignoring it completely as she raced after the warden and his men.

She overtook them two hours later along the river. They weren't at all hard to find. Jessie just followed the sounds of the barking dogs and the gunfire. When she caught up with the warden, he had already captured all but one of the fugitives.

"He's got a gun," the warden said. "Don't ask me how he got it, but he did. Shot two of my dogs and winged one of my best men."

"Any sign of Ki?"

"No," the warden said. "Nor of Ferrell Taggert."

Jessie looked off toward the trees. "I'd like to talk to that prisoner. Any chance of taking him alive?"

"I doubt it," the warden said. "He knows that he's got nothing to lose."

"Try and make him surrender," Jessie said. "It's important

116

because he might know something about Ki and Taggert."

"All right," the warden said, "but I won't risk the life of a single man. If this prisoner wants to go down fighting, there's nothing that we can do except oblige him."

The warden cupped his hands to his mouth and shouted. "No more firing! No more firing!"

Then he paused and yelled, "Prisoner, this is Warden Patrick Locke. Can you hear me?"

"Hell yes," the prisoner shouted from somewhere deep in the thick cottonwood trees that flanked the Carson River. "But we ain't got nothing to talk about!"

"Identify yourself!"

There was a long silence and then the prisoner shouted, "Matt Holland."

Locke frowned and then he pulled a little notebook from his shirt pocket, and quickly thumbed through it until he found Holland's name.

"You're in for armed robbery, Holland. That's no life sentence."

"It is in your prison!"

"You got just five years to go until you're eligible for probation. Five years isn't worth trading for a grave."

"I'm a dead man now, either way," Holland shouted. "I know it and so do you."

"No," Locke argued loudly. "You didn't plan that prison break. And you didn't kill any of my guards, did you?"

"Hell, don't try to bullshit me, Warden! I just shot one a few minutes ago! I tell you, I'm a dead man!"

"You winged one of the guards," Locke yelled. "That's not going to get you hanged."

"Yeah, well it ain't getting me a parole, either."

"Let's talk man to man," Locke shouted. "Just you and me."

Another long silence. "All right."

Locke took a deep breath. "But you've got to come out unarmed, same as me."

Holland laughed coarsely. "You must be crazy! I'm coming out with a gun in my fist. You can do the same if

117

you want. But I won't shoot unless you or your men open fire."

Locke sleeved sweat from his forehead. Jessie watched the warden for a moment as he mulled over the proposition, not liking it one little bit.

"Dave," he said, turning to his most trusted guard. "You get down low where he can't see you or your rifle. If he even looks like he wants to use that pistol, drop him."

Dave Rhine nodded and Jessie felt her heart pound faster. She had asked the warden to risk his life and now he was going to do it. She checked her own sixgun and flattened out on the ground. If the desperate prisoner was planning to take the warden's life, then, along with the guard, Jessie was going to try and stop him first.

"Here goes," the warden said, standing up straight with his gun in his fist pointing toward the earth.

As the warden started forward, every guard took a hidden firing position.

Jessie saw the escaped prisoner emerge warily from the trees. He was a tall, ragged-looking man with sunken cheeks and haunted eyes that darted from one direction to the other. Like the warden, Holland had a pistol clenched in his fist and it was also pointing downward.

The warden and the prisoner came to a halt about twenty yards apart. For a moment, neither man spoke. Then Warden Locke said, "If you drop the gun and cooperate by telling me who staged this prison breakout, I promise you there will be no punishment."

"I don't believe that," the prisoner said. "You'll throw me in solitary and have me on bread and water until I'm starved to death."

"I've never starved a prisoner in my entire career," Locke said. "You know that. Now drop that gun and tell me who's behind all this."

"I don't know."

"What happened to Taggert and prisoner Ki?"

"I don't know that either."

"They weren't among the prisoners we counted who didn't

escape and they weren't among those that we captured. I want to know where they are."

"I tell you, I don't know!"

The man's voice carried a note of rising hysteria. "And I can see you got men with their rifles pointed at me! I can see . . . four or five in the brush, all waiting to kill me."

"No!" Locke shouted. "They're under strict orders not to . . ."

But Holland wasn't listening. Maybe he saw yet another guard or something that triggered his panic because he suddenly lifted his gun and just managed to get it level before a volley of rifles belched smoke and death. The sound of Jessie's sixgun was drowned by the rifles and she saw the prisoner's chest, neck, and face dissolve in a red smear. Holland's body was hurled backward a good ten feet by the concerted impact of so many bullets.

Jessie lowered her own smoking gun. She did not need to look back up at the scene to know that the warden was unhurt and that the prisoner was dead.

Jessie walked heavily back to her gray mare and slowly remounted. She started to rein the horse south when the warden's voice stopped her.

"Hey, where the hell are you off to! Carson City is the other direction."

Jessie twisted around in her saddle to see the warden coming toward her. "I know where Carson City is," she said. "But I'm riding south, to Bullfrog."

"Don't," Locke said. "You'll only get yourself killed. I can send a telegram and maybe . . ."

"No," Jessie said. "Ki is my best friend. I'm going after him."

"You won't stand a chance against them," Warden Locke told her. "If you'd just wait until we could maybe form a posse or something, I'm sure we could handle things."

"Thanks, but no thanks," Jessie said.

And with that, she touched spurs to her horse and raced south toward a town called Bullfrog.

★

Chapter 18

They did not remove Ki's blindfold until they had ridden from sunrise to sundown. And when at last they halted to form a cold desert camp, Ki was again trussed hand and foot.

He looked up and saw a tall man and a young woman staring down at him in the glow of their campfire.

"When the food is ready," the man said, "your hands will be untied so that you can eat."

When Ki said nothing but turned his attention on the young woman, she shifted and said in a voice that could not be heard by the others, "We . . . we are sorry that you have to suffer but we have no choice."

"There is always a choice," Ki said quietly. "You could let me go."

"To do that would be to sign our own death warrants," the woman told him. "And like you, we are not ready to die."

The samurai stared at her so intently that she squirmed. "What is wrong?"

"Are you Judge Davis's niece?"

Her eyes widened with surprise. "How did you guess?"

"I can't tell you except to say that I am not what you think."

Allen's face reflected confusion. He grabbed the girl's

120

arm and pulled her away. "I was told you are dangerous. Already, I can see why."

"How come you voluntarily participated in that stage-coach robbery outside of Carson City when three men were killed, Miss Reynolds?"

She had started to walk away, but now she froze in her tracks before she slowly turned about and came back to stand over him. "I had no choice. He would have killed both of us."

"Who is 'he'?" the samurai pressed. "Tell me and I'll . . ."

"Alice, don't say another word!"

But the woman studied Ki very intently for a long moment. In her eyes, Ki read fear and confusion and something that struck him very much like a plea for help. Before Alice Reynolds turned her back to Ki, the samurai had the distinct impression she almost wanted to tell him who was really behind everything.

"From now on," Allen hissed, "you don't talk to her. I'm the only one that you say a word to. Is that clearly understood?"

Ki took a deep breath. "I understand you very well. You're as afraid as she is. I can actually smell your fear."

Allen opened his mouth to say something, but clamped it shut in silence and then he stomped away. Only later, when he returned to untie the samurai's wrists and give him food and water did he speak.

"You're going to be the death of us," Allen hissed. "And you were right about us living in fear. Is it any wonder? You're going to either escape, or be killed trying to escape and that will go very hard on me and the girl."

"Why?"

"Because the Boss Man made me responsible for returning with your hidden cache of gold."

"Why not help me escape? I'll make sure that you and the girl get away safe and then I'll see that the Boss Man as you call him is hunted down like a rabid dog. He'll either be shot, or hanged."

"Not very damned likely," Allen said. "The man is brilliant and he's utterly ruthless. I would never bet my life against him."

"You may have to," the samurai said, "whether you want to or not."

Allen pushed back. "You just lead us to that buried gold."

A thin smile formed on Ki's lips. "Why? So that you can take it all and bury me in the same hole?"

Allen sighed. "I could try and tell you that isn't the way it's supposed to happen, but you'd never believe me."

"That's true," Ki said.

"All right then," Allen said. "What if I told you that you had it figured correctly. That I do have orders to kill you after the gold has been recovered but that Alice and I have decided to risk defying those orders."

"Why?"

"Because we *aren't* killers," Allen said in a low voice.

"If an animal runs with a pack, he belongs to the pack," Ki said with calm reasoning. "And if he tries to leave the pack, they will kill him."

Allen threw his head back and gazed up at the stars. "When I became a mining engineer, I thought I would have bright, honorable future. I dreamed of discovering great mineral deposits that would elevate the lives of frontiersmen. What a fool I was!"

"How did you become ensnared by this man who controls you?"

Allen was silent for a long, long time. "I have a weakness for gambling," he said, unable to meet the samurai's eyes. "I simply cannot stop once I begin to lose. I keep thinking that the very next card, or the next hand, will be the one that will change my luck."

"But it never does?"

"No," Allen corrected, "once in a great while I have climbed out of a heavy loss to recoup myself. It has happened just often enough to make me think it will happen every time. And so, one night in Virginia City, I sold my soul and my future to the devil."

"I see," Ki said. "And this debt that you are under, it will never be repaid, will it?"

Allen's head snapped up. "If I am successful in returning to my . . . my employer the ten thousand dollars in gold you have buried in Bullfrog . . . and if I help my employer strike it rich at our mine, then I will have more than repaid my debt."

"No," Ki argued. "You are trapped in this man's web. You will never be free."

"Don't say that," the engineer whispered, despair heavy in his voice. "I *will* be free never again to became enslaved by the roll of the dice or the turn of a card."

"I am your only hope of escape," Ki told the man in a flat, uncompromising voice. "I know you do not yet believe that, but by the time that we reach Bullfrog, it will be apparent. And by then, you will have to make a decision to help me."

"Finish eating," Allen demanded. "I do not trust Miss Reynolds out of my sight for a moment with those men."

Ki looked over at the girl who was sitting apart from the gang, which numbered seven. These were hard, cruel men and Ki had no doubt that any one of them might well be plotting to keep the buried gold for themselves—if it existed.

For the next five days they rode steadily south. In the summertime the heat would have been punishing, but during the winter it was pleasant enough. The gang members spoke little and every time Ki thought that he might be given a chance to escape, one of the gang was watching him closely. As for Allen and the girl, the farther south they rode, the more morose the pair became. Ki could only wonder if they were beginning to realize that their only hope was in helping him.

One of the men in particular seemed to never take his eyes off the samurai. This was a dirty and unkempt member of the gang named Shorty Lee. The man stood only a little over five feet tall and could not have weighed one hundred twenty pounds soaking wet. He wore a Stetson that was so

123

large that it looked ridiculous on his head, and two sixguns were strapped to his skinny hips and they too looked over-sized on the little man. To top it off, Shorty Lee liked to clean his tobacco-stained teeth with a huge Bowie knife.

Shorty would have been a mere oddity expect for one thing—he had an extremely annoying habit of humming the same unknown tune over and over until even Ki found it getting on his nerves.

"Can't you hum some other goddamn tune?" one of the men finally demanded.

"Uh-uh."

"Well why the hell not!"

" 'Cause this one is the only one I like," Lee informed the man.

"Well it's drivin' all of us about half loco!"

In answer, Lee just hummed a bit louder. This went on for about a mile until another man sided with the first in demanding that Lee be silent.

"Shorty, either hum something else, or shut the hell up!"

Shorty stopped humming, but just when everyone was about to feel relieved, Shorty said, "You two boys say you don't like my hummin', huh?"

"You sure got that right."

Lee reined his horse up and before Ki or anyone else quite expected it, Shorty yanked both of his big guns and cut down his detractors with four of the quickest bullets that Ki had ever seen fired by any man.

"Jezus!" Allen shouted. "What the hell is wrong with you!"

In reply, Shorty simply turned his guns on Allen and grinned. "You don't like the way I settle my troubles, say so now."

Allen's face drained and he could barely speak he was so scared. "No," he managed to croak. "I got no problem with you, Shorty. It's just that you didn't have to kill them."

"Yeah I did," Shorty said, guns still clenched in his little fists. "You like my hummin' okay, Allen?"

"Why . . . why sure!"

Shorty seemed pleased. He looked to the others whose heads began to rapidly bob up and down.

Satisfied, the little killer finally reloaded and then holstered his guns.

The girl swallowed and Ki heard her say, "Allen, we can't just leave those two men lying in the road dead like that."

"Well, what are we supposed to do with them?"

"We can tie them across their saddles and take them onto the next town and pay someone to bury them."

"Yeah," Allen said, dismounting from his horse. "Come on some of you men, help me."

But no one gave any indication they intended to help. Shorty Lee began to clean his teeth with the Bowie knife and the other men just sat on their horses looking off into the distance.

"Untie my wrists and I'll help," Ki offered in a soft voice.

Allen nodded and started to move toward the samurai, but Shorty spurred his horse between them.

"You leave them two to rot out here," the little man ordered. "We got no time for messin' round with nonsense. We got gold to pack and might be we can use those two extra saddle horses."

Allen wanted to protest but he didn't and Ki thought he saw the spark of keen disappointment in Alice Reynolds's eyes.

"All right," Allen said, trying to make it sound like he and not Shorty was in charge of all the decisions. "Let's ride on. Bullfrog can't be but another twenty or thirty miles farther."

No one said much to that so they continued on and Shorty began to hum again. For his part, the samurai studied the little man with new interest. He'd already sized up these outlaws, but Shorty had been the last one of them that had seemed to be a real threat.

He's the ringer of the bunch, Ki thought. And it's a good thing this happened or I might have made the fatal mistake of underestimating him.

125

Just about sundown that evening, they topped a low rise of hills and stared out at an immense high-desert valley at least twenty miles long and seven miles wide. The valley was treeless and foreboding and the road they were following led directly down its center.

"Unless we been misguided," Allen said, "that's Bull-frog."

"It sure ain't much, is it," one of the man swore because there could not have been more than twenty buildings altogether.

"Where's the gold buried?" Shorty asked, turning to focus his attention on the samurai.

Ki raised his finger and pointed across the valley. "I'm afraid that I buried it at the south end. Be another twenty-five miles or so."

"We've ridden this far," Shorty said, "a few more miles one way or the other won't matter. Just as long as it's where you say it is."

"Of course," said Ki.

Shorty seemed to look right through him, but the little man kept his silence.

"It's almost sundown," Allen said. "Our horses are hungry and we need water. I expect we can find what we need down there and we can go the rest of the way tomorrow morning."

The weary outlaws nodded, and when Allen kicked his horse forward toward Bullfrog everyone followed, Shorty bringing up the rear beside Ki.

"You're thinking that you finally got a good chance of escapin', aren't you?" Shorty asked with a smile that chilled the samurai's blood.

"Nope. Escape never entered my mind."

"You're a damned liar," Shorty said. "And you know what?"

When Ki didn't respond, Shorty hissed, "I'm thinking you done pulled the wool over the Boss Man's eyes. I don't think there's any gold a'tall."

Ki knew that the little killer was reading his expression,

and so the samurai showed no emotion when he said, "We'll see about that in the morning, won't we?"

"You damn right," Shorty said, "and if I'm right, you're gonna die as hard as any man ever died. I got a little Apache blood in me, you know. Gives me my courage and my meanness."

Ferrell Taggert, who was not a talkative man, finally could hold his silence no longer. "Listen Shorty, I know this man from prison and I'm damn sure not about to get fooled. He killed a prospector by the name of Jeb Mason and he took his gold."

"Oh, says who!"

"He did, dammit!" Taggert twisted around to Ki. "How much is that buried gold worth?"

"A hell of a lot more than the ten thousand that I agreed to pay you."

"Ha!" Shorty snorted. "Well in case you ain't figured it out, you're going to pay us all of it!"

Ki glared at the little killer. "I figured it out all right. But if it gets me out of thirty years in the Nevada State Prison, then it'll be worth everything. I just figure to come out of this with my hide."

"You will," Taggert vowed. "I give you my word on that."

"You shouldn't ever make promises you can't keep," Shorty said.

"You snake-like sonofabitch," Taggert hissed. "You might be fast on the trigger, but I ain't afraid of you."

"You should be, but you never was long on brains," Shorty said, goading the man.

Taggert's eyes shuttered. "You and me," he said. "The day is coming. And when it does, you'll be the one that is left layin' in the dust."

"Don't count on it, Ferrell. And if your China boy here don't come though with the gold, you and him will both die long and slow. And that's *my* promise. You both better understand that right now."

In answer, Taggert spat tobacco juice in the dust before

127

he spurred his horse on up ahead. When Shorty challenged Allen and the young woman to interfere, they looked away, faces strained in silence.

Ki kept his eyes straight ahead. He could hear Shorty Lee chuckling to himself as they rode on toward Bullfrog.

Ki knew that one thing and one thing only was for certain—tonight was his last real chance to escape. It was pointless to wait any longer for Allen or Miss Reynolds to help him. And he had the feeling that, when it came right down to it, Taggert wasn't going to risk his life either against a faster gun.

No, Ki thought, sizing up his own dismal circumstances, I will have to either do it on my own, or I am buzzard bait, just like the two dead outlaws Shorty had killed and whose bones were probably already being picked clean.

★

Chapter 19

Jessie reined her sweat-drenched dapple mare to a standstill and let the animal catch its wind. She watched a pair of dust devils dance across the valley floor toward a distant mining settlement.

The settlement appeared to be quite large, with a main street and numerous side streets. Jessie could see three or four hoisting works and a lot of tailings which indicated that Bullfrog was a very active mining community. A procession of ore wagons was leaving the town heading south toward the still distant Colorado River.

"That's it," Jessie sighed. "That *has* to be Bullfrog."

The mare had proven its mettle on the long, hard ride down from the Carson Valley. Jessie had ridden the poor horse more than sixteen hours a day, pausing only to sleep for a few hours at night and to rest when the mare's strength began to flag.

As she was about to move on, something caught her eye off a few miles to the right, and she stiffened in her saddle. Horsemen. Seven or eight of them and they were moving south at a steady trot toward the distant mining town.

"It might be them," she whispered through dry, cracked lips. "It *has* to be them!"

Jessie wished she had a pair of binoculars but, failing that, she knew exactly what was required. She would wait until the riders were several miles ahead of her, and then she would fall behind and follow them into the mining town.

Waiting, however, was difficult. Jessie had ridden so hard that even the mare seemed upset at stopping so near water and feed.

"Fifteen minutes," Jessie said, dismounting, her green eyes never once leaving the distant body of horsemen. "And then we go after them."

When a quarter of an hour had passed, Jessie remounted and put the mare to a hard gallop. Very soon, she detected the horsemen's trail and fell into line with them as they moved toward Bullfrog.

The sun was dipping behind the eastern hills, drenching the land with brilliant sundown colors when Jessie rode into Bullfrog. She found a water trough attended to by an old Chinaman.

"One cent you drink, ten cents for your horse to drink, missy," the old man said, bowing respectfully.

Jessie understood. Either the water had to be hauled in from a great distance by wagon trains, or else there was a well somewhere about that required a great deal of effort to bring up the water. Obviously, the Chinaman expected to be rewarded for his efforts.

Jessie paid the old man ten cents. "Have you seen many riders come in from that direction?" she asked, pointing back to the north.

The old man nodded and watched as Jessie's mare inhaled the water in huge gulps.

"Where did they go?"

"Information ten cents, missy."

Jessie paid the old Chinaman. "Now, it's important. Did they ride on through town or stop for the night."

"They stop. Go livery at other end of Bullfrog. Look very bad, missy."

"Did you notice that one of them was an Oriental . . . like yourself only different."

The old man frowned and Jessie tried to explain things

130

a little better. "He would have been wearing a black tunic, a braided leather headband, and sandals just like you are wearing. Did you see this one riding with those men?"

The Chinaman smiled. He extended his hand, palm upward.

Jessie dropped a quarter into the thin, calloused palm.

"Yes missy. The one you seek was among them. He looked very sad."

Jessie relaxed visibly. Her entire body sagged with relief. "Then I am not too late," she whispered to herself.

"I take horse, find hay, and brush for a dollar," the Chinaman said hopefully.

"I might need this horse very suddenly," Jessie said. "And if I could not find her, then I would be very angry with you. Very, very angry. I would cut off that queue of yours."

The Chinaman's rheumy old eyes dilated with concern. "I would not steal horse. I live over there. I have corral and good hay."

Jessie was anxious to be free of the mare and to go after Ki and his abductors. There was no other livery in sight and she was too preocuppied with saving Ki to want to search for one.

"All right," she told the Chinaman. Jessie reached into her pants pocket and fished out a dollar. "I want you to take my horse over to your house and feed it all that it can eat. And I want you to stay with the horse until I need it. Do you understand?"

The Chinaman stared at the dollar as his head vigorously bobbed up and down.

"Good," Jessie said, untying her saddlebags and yanking her Winchester from its boot. Jessie had a long coat which had served her well during the cold nights on the trail and now she pulled it on. With the knee-length coat and with her hair tucked under her hat, she knew that she would be taken for just another drifter that had arrived in town, maybe seeking work in one of the local mines.

She headed up the street, covered with dust and hat pulled down low over her brow. She had no idea where the Black

Bandana Gang would take Ki but the first place to start would be at the livery where they had boarded their weary horses.

No one paid Jessie any attention as she traversed Bullfrog. The day's activity was winding down and there were only a few horses and ore wagons still moving up and down the street. Most of the business had now moved into the numerous saloons that lined the main thoroughfare.

When Jessie finally reached the livery, she moved very cautiously, afraid that she might run into the gang and provoke gunfire. Over and over, she reminded herself that no one in the gang would recognize her, certainly not Ferrell Taggert.

"Afternoon, mister," the liveryman said as he pitched hay into a corral of still sweaty horses. "Can I help you?"

"I hope so," Jessie said, lowering her voice to sound like a man. "I'm looking to buy a horse. And I see that you've got plenty here."

"Oh, these aren't mine to sell," the liveryman said, the pitchfork coming to a rest in his hands as he stared at Jessie. "Say, are you a woman?"

There was no point in denying the fact because Jessie knew that, even with the long coat and her hair hidden up under her hat, her voice had given her away. "I am. But I still need a horse."

"Well I'll be damned," the liveryman said with a grin. "You almost had me fooled. So what's a woman like you needing a horse for? There's a stageline that rolls in and out of Bullfrog twice a week to points north and south."

"Maybe I need a horse to go prospecting," Jessie said, knowing the comment sounded slightly ridiculous.

"Well if you want to prospect, you need a burro, not a horse," the man said, turning his full attention on her. "A horse will plumb starve to death out in those hills. He'll drink twice the water that a burro will and he can't take the heat, either."

"Oh." Jessie moved over to the corral. "These horses look hard-used."

132

"They have been. It was a rough bunch that rode them in here less than an hour ago. So rough that I asked them to pay me a day's board in advance. I don't usually do that, but all the hay in Bullfrog has to be shipped in on wagons and this many horses could eat up a month's profits real quick."

"I understand. Do you think that one of the men who rode these horses into town might be willing to sell one for a fair price."

"You'd have to ask them," the liveryman said, returning to his work. "But I still say that if you really mean to prospect a burro is the ticket."

"You can't ride a burro," Jessie said.

The liveryman chuckled and looked up at her with a grin. "Lady, I don't know what your game is, but I'm not interested. You're no more interested in buying a horse or a burro than I am in visiting the man in the moon."

"What makes you so sure of that?"

The liveryman pitched the last of his hay into the corral before he turned and answered. "Because you got a pretty face and pretty hands. Hands that have never held a pick or shovel and a face that ain't used to this desert heat, sun, and wind. What do you really want to know?"

"Want to know where the men that own these horses have gone."

"Why didn't you just come out and say so in the first place?"

"I have my reasons."

"They went to find a room at the Miner's Hotel, and I suggested the best food was to be had at the Granite Café right next door."

"Thanks."

Jessie started to turn and walk away, but the man stopped her when he said, "One of them men your husband or something?"

"No. My friend."

"The one that had his hands tied up?"

Jessie nodded. "You noticed, huh?"

133

"Hard not to notice. It wasn't all that easy for him to dismount and they kept a mighty close eye on him. He looked to me to be in a hell of a bad fix."

"Thanks for the information."

"You want my advice, you'll steer clear of that bunch. They mean business and you'd better understand that the nearest law is down over in Beatty. Sheriff Manse is his name, but he ain't too interested in doing much more than locking up drunks."

"I'll remember that," Jessie said as she walked away.

★

Chapter 20

Jessie had no trouble finding the Miner's Hotel, but since it was for men only and she would have caused a stir had she entered, Jessie went across the street to the Granite Café. Despite its being busy and almost full, Jessie was lucky enough to find a little table against the back of the room, and she was careful to keep her hat pulled down low.

"What'll it be, mister?" a harried man in a greasy apron demanded.

"Steak and potatoes. Coffee to drink," Jessie growled.

The man hurried away after taking Jessie's order. Several minutes later, her coffee was smacked down in front of her. "Forgot to ask. How you like your steak?"

"Medium."

"Okay."

Jessie swiveled around in her chair and was happy to see that no one was paying her any attention. She was the only woman in the café, which obviously catered to a rough crowd of miners and freighters.

Her steak and potatoes arrived in less than five minutes. The steak was tough and it oozed blood when Jessie sawed into it, but she wasn't complaining. She'd had damn poor fare on the way south and she had to hold herself in check in order not to wolf her food down.

She was on her third bite of the rubbery steak when the door opened and she saw Ki, surrounded by a knot of hard cases and a rather pretty young woman. Jessie was so shocked to see a woman with the men that she had to force-feed herself for a minute while she gathered her wits. Was this Judge Davis's missing niece? Jessie was sure that it was.

Appetite suddenly gone, Jessie kept her head down and watched the man who'd served her go over to the group and say, "I'm afraid you got here a little late. You could try the Stone Cup Café just down the street, or come back in about an hour when I've got a few empty tables."

"Mister," a short, dirty member of the gang said, "we want to eat *now*."

"I'm sorry. But like I just explained . . ."

The short man turned to the nearest table where six hungry miners were seated. "You boys are just finishin', ain't you," he said.

One of the miners, a big, redheaded man with a red checkered shirt, looked up and said, "Hell, we just ordered!"

"Steaks?"

"Yeah, but what the hell is it to you?"

The short man drew his gun and jammed it into the big miner's throat so fast that Jessie blinked just to make sure she had seen properly.

"Steaks will do just dandy," the short man said, "and that will save us some time. Now git before my thumb slips off this hammer and I blow a hole through your gullet."

The redheaded miner managed to nod his head. "Sure thing, fella," he gulped.

But one of the other miners wasn't ready to leave the table without a fight. Jessie saw the man reach down and slowly extract a derringer from his boot top. The miner's hand and legs were hidden under the table and Jessie held her breath as the derringer inched up close to his waist. There was no way for the short gunman to see the derringer.

"Well, wait a minute," the man with the derringer said in mild protest. "Now don't you think this is a little bit unfair?"

136

Shorty Lee snickered. "Life is unfair. Git!"

The miner jerked his derringer up with a curse on his lips. He fired at the very same instant that Shorty fired but there was one very significant difference—Shorty Lee didn't miss.

The miner slapped at his forehead as if he had been stung by a hornet and Jessie saw his eyes cross an instant later as blood poured out from between his fingers.

The young woman beside Ki turned away and rushed out the door. Jessie heard her vomiting in the street as another man quickly followed her outside. Other than those two, nobody moved as the miner's hands dropped to his sides and he rolled out of his chair to sprawl dead across the floor.

"Anyone else got any surprises?" Shorty asked, waving the barrel of his gun in front of the other miners who shook their heads.

"Then git!"

The miners grabbed their dead friend by the boots and quickly dragged him out the door.

"Sit down and eat!" Shorty Lee exclaimed with a wide smile. "Steaks comin' up."

The man with the apron stammered, "How you . . . you like yours, sir?"

"Rare," Shorty said, wiping the dead miner's blood off the table from in front of him. "Bloody rare!"

Jessie shivered as the little man cackled. She had seen men like this one before, but there were far and few between and they rarely lived to full maturity.

Ki saw her. Jessie's eyes locked with those of the samurai and she tried but failed to smile encouragingly. For his part, the samurai shook his head back and forth so imperceptibly that no one but she would notice.

What was he trying to tell her? That he did not want her help? Jessie was stubborn enough to nod her head up and down in defiance. She wanted her friend to know that he had played his lone hand plenty long enough. She had agreed to let him go into that terrible prison and then put himself at the mercy of first the prisoners, then this ruthless gang.

But enough. Like it or not, she was going to help him. After all, she thought, what did he think she had ridden all the way down from Carson City for, to watch a man die at a café table?

Hell no.

Jessie managed to finish her meal knowing that she was already weak from too much riding and too little sleep and food. Without attracting attention, she paid her bill, keenly aware that Ki was watching her every movement.

As she was passing by the samurai on her way outside, she heard one of the men say, "We better keep a watch tonight or some of them miners might try and get even."

"Not very damn likely," another said, "not after the way that Shorty handled his gun."

The samurai's eyes watched Jessie until she disappeared. It had been decided that his hands and legs would be untied so that he did not attract any more attention than he'd already received. But Ki knew that the moment he was taken upstairs to their rooms in the Miner's Hotel he would again be bound hand and foot. That being the case, the logical thing to do was to make his escape before he was forced to reenter the hotel.

Ki hardly listened to the conversations of the men who surrounded him at their table. He did note that the other diners, despite being rough working men accustomed to death and injury, acted subdued by the chilling violence they'd just witnessed. They ate quickly and mostly in silence before paying their bills and leaving in a hurry.

Allen and Alice did not return to the café and Ki wrote them off entirely. They might, he thought, even have sneaked back to their horses and run away together. No matter. He was sure that he could not have trusted them and they would probably have gotten themselves killed needlessly if they'd have tried to intervene to save his life.

Ferrell Taggert ate in stony silence. Ki noticed that the escaped prisoner didn't meet anyone's eyes and he acted subdued. The samurai was sure that the man had completely lost his nerve and was afraid of being killed by Shorty tomorrow morning when they supposedly unearthed the buried prospector's gold.

And finally, as the samurai ate, he thought about Jessie. On the one hand, he was filled with new hope and gratitude because she possessed enough brains, cunning, and skill to help him escape. On the other hand, he was worried that she might also be killed and that made the samurai angry at himself for not escaping earlier.

"Let's get out of here," Shorty said when he finished eating.

No one argued. They spilled a few dollars on the table, not bothering to count to see if it was enough, then they filed out the door. Ki was marched across the street and into the lobby of the hotel.

There wasn't a hope of escape. He had men all around him, and Shorty, who could draw and fire in the bat of an eye, was careful to stay well behind, so that the samurai had no chance of delivering a foot or hand strike.

The samurai did not see Jessie anywhere as he was marched up the stairs to their rooms.

"Where do you suppose that Allen and the girl went off to?" Taggert said, breaking a long silence.

"He's probably down the hall puttin' the meat to her," one of the gang chuckled.

No one laughed.

"My guess is that they ran out on us," Shorty told no one in particular. "They haven't the guts for this business."

"What the hell do we do about it?" Taggert blurted out. "You know the Boss Man needs him at the mine."

"The hell with them both," Shorty hissed. "If Allen is so valuable, the Boss Man shouldn't have sent him along with us. Let him worry about the mine. All I'm thinking about is that gold we're supposed to dig up tomorrow morning. Isn't that right, Chinaman?"

139

Ki looked right through the little man. Without a gun, Shorty Lee was nothing.

"I said, isn't that right!" Shorty snarled.

Ki did not blink, not even when the back of the little killer's hand struck him on the cheek and knocked him a step backward.

"I'd kill you right now if it wasn't for the fact that you just might not be lying," Shorty said. "That, and the fact that—if you are lying—I'm going to enjoy staking you out on the desert floor and skinning you alive."

The samurai showed no fear and Shorty Lee must have appreciated his courage because he said, "Maybe you even got some Apache courage in you. Maybe some warriors screwed your Chinese mother and you was born a bastard, huh?"

When Ki said nothing, Shorty drew his pistol and pointed it at his heart.

"What the hell are you doing!" Taggert cried. "You gone completely loco!"

Shorty pivoted and cocked back the hammer of his gun. "What the hell," he said, "why wait to have all my fun tomorrow morning. Why not start the party right now."

"What . . . what do you mean?" Taggert cried, his face draining of blood.

"I mean," Shorty said, enjoying himself hugely, "that you had better go for your gun."

"Now! With you already fillin' your hand?"

"All right." Shorty holstered his Colt and his little fingers flexed and unflexed. "Go for it right now, Ferrell. Let's see what you got."

Ferrell began to wag his head back and forth. "Now wait a minute," he said, voice pleading. "This is crazy. We got orders from the Boss Man to find that gold and bring it back."

"But one of us ain't comin' back," Shorty said, sounding very patient, as if he were explaining something complex to a child. "Don't you see that yet?"

"But . . ."

140

"Draw, damn you coward!" Shorty shrieked.

Ferrell, to his small credit, drew. But he was so unnerved that he bungled the effort and when Shorty's gun came up, Ferrell Taggert screamed and the gun fell from his hand to clatter on the floor.

"Don't kill me!"

"Beg. Get down on your knees and beg for your life."

Ki looked away. The sight of Taggert collapsing to his knees made the samurai sick in his heart. No matter that Taggert was a killer. He was still a man and he retained a sense of honor in his desire to see that the samurai at least lived if he had fulfilled his part of the deal.

"Please," Taggert said, clasping his hands overhead and pleading. "Please don't kill me."

Shorty looked to the other members of the gang who gazed on impassively. "What do you boys think? Does he look like a man who has the guts to ride with the Black Bandana Gang?"

"He looks like a weeping old woman," one of them said with disgust. "He makes my stomach turn."

"Mine too," another man said, licking his lips nervously. "I think you ought to kill him like you did that miner, Shorty."

Shorty shrugged his narrow shoulders. "You heard them, Ferrell. They think you don't deserve to live. They think you've disgraced yourself. I agree."

"No!"

Shorty surprised everyone by holstering his gun. "I'm going to give you your life, Ferrell. But if you cross me even once I'll cut your throat from ear to ear."

The samurai heard Ferrell's broken sob of relief and then he heard Shorty chortle and break into a full belly laugh.

★

Chapter 21

Jessie did not sleep much at all that night. In the morning, she could feel her eyes sting, and her head felt as if it were stuffed with desert sand. It was still dark outside but Jessie knew that it was very close to sunrise. Yet having no idea how or when she was going to try and save her samurai, Jessie dressed by candlelight. Scooping up her saddlebags and Winchester, she headed off to find her dapple mare and to prepare for whatever kind of deadly confrontation the morning would bring.

There were a few ore wagons and miners moving quietly on the street when Jessie made her way to the Chinaman's hut. She found her saddle beside the old man's corral and she had no difficulty catching up to the dapple-gray mare.

Jessie saddled the animal quickly. "I hope that you ate better than I did last night," she said. "And that you feel more rested."

In answer, the mare nuzzled her cheek and, somehow, the act lifted Jessie's flagging spirits.

When the mare was saddled, Jessie led her up the street and tied her across from the Miner's Hotel. Then, with nothing better to do, she sat down on the boardwalk with her rifle resting across her knees. She pulled her Stetson down low to the rising sun and prepared to wait and see

142

how the morning would unfold. One thing Jessie had vowed to herself was not to allow them to take the samurai out of Bullfrog.

On this main street, she reasoned, with townspeople all around, at least she would have witnesses. Maybe someone would even take up the fight when they realized that she was a woman against seasoned gunmen. But no matter. Out in the middle of a desert, she would have no chance whatsoever either of saving Ki, or of saving herself.

Bullfrog, Jessie knew, was where she had to make her stand. Jessie was sure that Ki would have reached the same conclusion and that he would act when the moment of decision arrived.

It was still quite early when Jessie saw the Black Bandana Gang lead Ki outside. Alice Reynolds and a tall young man seemed to be holding back as they started down the street toward the livery.

Jessie waited until they were moving along, then she fell in unnoticed behind them. Coiled tighter than a spring, Jessie made the decision to wait until the men she followed reached the corral and were occupied with saddling their horses before she initiated a confrontation that would inevitably lead to bloodshed, quite likely her own. Also, she was not at all sure that the samurai knew she was trailing along behind.

When they came to the corral, there was little conversation. One man kept a sharp eye on the samurai while the others began to catch up to their horses and haul their saddles, bridles, and blankets out of the barn.

Jessie moved over to the nearest building. Ki saw her now and he knew that she was about to act in his behalf. Maybe that was why the samurai decided not to wait for Jessie but instead to act himself despite the fact that his wrists were bound together.

Jessie saw the samurai's hands slip inside his tunic and she saw the flash of his *shuriken* star blade as it cut through the bonds around his wrists. His guard, who had been momentarily distracted by the bucking of one of the

143

horses, had no chance at all as the samurai chopped the iron-hard edge of his hand down against the base of his captor's neck. The man dropped as if he had been shot.

Jessie stepped out from behind cover and levered a shell into her Winchester. "All of you, freeze!"

Shorty Lee's hand streaked for the big gun on his hip but never reached it as Jessie's first slug caught him squarely in the chest and flung him back into the corral.

One of the gang shouted a belated warning and then everyone was either running for cover or reaching for their sidearms. Jessie shot another man in the belly and he began to scream. She saw the young woman and the man who had been holding her arm make a dash for safety but a bullet dropped the man and the woman fell on him crying.

The samurai, free at last, became a killing machine. His first *shuriken* star blade brought one outlaw to his knees staring at his chest and a second member of the gang managed to get off one bullet before the samurai kicked him backward into the plunging horses where he was trampled beyond recognition.

Ferrell Taggert bolted and ran but Ki's voice stopped him in his tracks when he yelled, "Hold it!"

Ferrell, his gun clenched in his fist, whirled around. His face was a mask of hatred. "You lied to me! Right from the start, you lied about everything! The gold, the prospector, everything!"

Ki took a step forward and Jessie levered a fresh shell into her rifle. The samurai raised a hand and said, "Drop the gun and you go back to prison. Raise it and you go to the cemetery."

"I ain't goin' back to prison!"

Ki expelled a deep breath. His fingers slipped into his tunic and Jessie knew that he had one more hidden star blade. "Ferrell, you tried to stand up for me. I don't want to see you die. Drop the gun."

"No!" the man bellowed, dragging his gun up.

Ki's arm lashed forward and, as Jessie fired her rifle, she saw the star blade strike Taggert in the forehead and then her own bullet kicked him back into the corral. The horses, crazed by the shooting and the smell of fresh blood, poured out of the corral and stampeded down the main street of Bullfrog.

"Are you all right?" Jessie cried, running to Ki's side.

"Yeah, but I'm afraid that he isn't."

Jessie and Ki hurried over to the girl and the fallen engineer. Jessie took one look at the spreading stain of blood on the tall man's shirt and knew that he was badly wounded.

"Let's find a doctor!" she said as townspeople began to emerge on the street, many still only half dressed.

"We need a doctor here!" Ki shouted.

Jessie unbuttoned the engineer's shirt and pulled it back to examine the wound.

"Is he going to die?" Alice Reynolds managed to ask, her eyes filled with tears.

"I can't say," Jessie replied, her practiced fingers gently probing the wound and trying to assess the internal damage.

The slug had entered just below the young man's ribs and, from the angle, Jessie thought it would be lucky indeed if the bullet had not pierced some vital organ.

"Make way! Make way!" a man shouted as he rushed to their side.

"Are you the town doctor?"

"I'm a dentist! But I'm all there is in Bullfrog. Let's get this man to my office."

Twenty minutes later, Jessie and the dentist were up to their elbows in blood as they extracted the bullet.

"He's still breathing," the dentist said, "and that's a good sign."

"I think he's going to live," Jessie told Judge Davis's niece. "I think he's going to make it if he can get through the next twenty-four hours."

Alice bent her head, covered her face, and wept uncontrollably. Later, Jessie would ask her all about the Black Bandana Gang and where its leader could be found.

Later, but not until her young lover was either dead or on the road to recovery.

It actually took two days before anyone could say whether or not the young man was going to survive. But at the end of that time Alice was all smiles, and Jessie knew she could wait no longer for the answers to her questions.

"Who is he?" she asked. "What is the name of the man behind the Black Bandana Gang?"

"His name is Hastings Long," Alice said. "But no one in our camp ever called him anything but the 'Boss Man.' "

"Hastings Long?" Jessie frowned. "Wasn't he a prominent figure involved in something unsavory a few years ago?"

Alice nodded. "He was a bright young attorney and then a county judge up in Virginia City. It was said that he would one day be governor of the State of Nevada and a United States senator."

"Yes," Jessie said. "I think he had money, too."

"That's true. He had everything. Money, family, connections, and he was bright. I think that I was in love with him when I was a girl. But later, when he was caught taking a huge bribe to overturn the conviction of a bank embezzler, he fell from grace. He was stripped of his office and even his family disowned him."

"Ahh, yes," Jessie said, "I remember reading about it even in the Texas papers. Everyone wondered why such a promising young man would take such a foolish risk."

"He is incredibly greedy and power hungry," Alice said. "He wants to be rich and go beyond state politics. His ambitions have no bounds."

Alice looked down at the young engineer. "And so, he organized the Black Bandana Gang and began killing and extorting whomever he could that would serve his purposes."

"And your young friend here?"

"He's cursed with gambling fever," Alice said. "He was easily enough lured into hopeless debt."

"I see."

146

"What will become of him?" Alice blurted. "He was a part of the gang—as I was—but never willingly. Will we be sent to prison?"

"I doubt it," Jessie said. "But may I suggest that as soon as Allen is fit to travel that you get married and take an extended honeymoon in California?"

Alice nodded vigorously and so did her young engineer, who added, "What about Hastings Long?"

"We'll need directions to that canyon," Ki said. "Other than that, it's no longer your concern."

"Directions?" Allen whispered in a weak voice. "Give me a paper and pencil and I'll draw you a map."

Jessie was two steps ahead of them and had anticipated his request, bringing writing materials.

As the wounded engineer began to sketch, he said, "Long has a major mining operation in that canyon."

"Is it producing?"

"Not yet," Allen said, "but it will. I was forced to work off my debt to him, but I knew from the start that he would strike the Comstock Lode if he didn't run out of operating capital first."

"Is that why he kept his men robbing banks, trains, and stagecoaches?"

"Yeah," Allen said, "He's probably got over a hundred thousand dollars invested in his mine, but when it finally strikes the big vein of ore down below, he stands to recoup his investment a dozen times over."

"If he does," Jessie said, "I'm sure that a lot of the profits will go back to reimbursing whomever he has robbed as well as the widows and orphaned children that he has left behind."

"Watch out for him," Allen said, gripping Jessie's hand. "He's a monster. The most cunning and diabolical man I've ever known. Don't let your guard down in his presence, even for a moment."

"Not a chance," Jessie said, climbing out of the bedside chair where she'd been sitting. "Goodbye."

"Will we ever see you again?" Alice asked.

147

"I don't know. But if I were you, I would change my name and find another line of work. After all, you both did ride with the Black Bandana Gang and it might be impossible to convince a jury that you had no alternatives."

"That's the truth of it, though," Allen said. "I swear that it is. Neither of us ever shot anyone."

"I believe you," Jessie said. "But I'd still find a new name and new life."

"We will," Alice promised. "And thank you!"

Jessie smiled and, together with her samurai, she left the dentist's office and headed outside as she tucked Allen's map in her shirt pocket.

Ki said nothing. All the talking was over and there was only one last piece of this nasty business that remained.

Hastings Long, "Boss Man."

That evening, Ki was feeling tense and restless so he went for a walk by himself. He was lost in thought when, suddenly, a young woman came running out from between two buildings and nearly collided with the samurai. She was disheveled and her dress was torn down to her waist revealing a pair of large, heaving breasts.

"Help!" she cried as a big man grabbed her arm and tried to pull her back into the shadows toward an alley. "Please, mister, help me!"

The samurai did not waste time asking idle questions. Instead, he jumped into the fray. He delivered a snap kick to the man's belly which slammed him up against the building and before the man could reach for the gun at his side, Ki delivered two crunching blows with the edge of his hand. The big man dropped like a felled tree.

"Oh thank you!" the young woman exclaimed, her eyes wide with wonder. She smiled, looked the samurai up and down. "How did you do that so easily?"

Ki shrugged. Standing in between the buildings he was embarrassed because he could not tear his eyes from the young woman's heaving breasts.

"You didn't kill him, did you?" the woman asked, looking down at the unconscious man.

"No," the samurai said with assurance. "He'll come around in a few hours."

"That's good." She followed his eyes to her breasts. "You seem a little distracted by something."

"I am," he admitted.

She cupped her breasts in her hands. "By these?"

Ki swallowed and nodded his head.

She blew a wisp of blond hair from her eyes. "You look like a man who has not had a woman in a long, long time."

"Do I?"

"Yes." The young woman stepped up close to the samurai and pressed herself to his body. "I've never had a total stranger come to my aid before. It makes me feel . . . like someone kinda special."

Ki lowered his face to the inviting breasts. "You are special," he said, tongue darting out to lave a nipple.

She moaned with pleasure and ground her hips against those of the samurai. "I am the mayor's daughter," she said. "And the man you just whipped has been trying to marry me for a long time but I don't love him."

"Then don't marry him," Ki said, licking the nipples and watching as they grew hard.

"But he *is* a very good lover," she whispered. "And I'll bet you are too."

Ki could feel his heart pounding in his chest. He knew it was crazy but he wanted this girl and he wanted her right now. Ki reached down and pulled her dress up and his long fingers found her womanhood.

"This is crazy," she breathed, clinging to the samurai as he struggled to relieve her of her undergarments. "I don't know your name. I don't know a single thing about you except that you are strong and very brave."

"Sometimes," Ki said, dropping his own pants and lifting the young woman up against the wall, "that's enough."

She spread her legs wide and the woman purred like a cat, then started rolling her shoulders from side to side, breasts brushing back and forth across the samurai's open mouth. Arching her back, she locked her legs around the samurai's waist and then cried out with pleasure as he impaled her with his throbbing manhood.

"I'm going to get splinters in my backside against this damned old wall and I don't even care," she panted, her bottom twitching and banging against Ki as she pulled him into her hot, wet depths.

Ki cradled her surprisingly muscular buttocks and thrust with mounting pleasure.

"This is insane," she whispered, voice hoarse with passion as she turned her head sideways and gazed up the corridor toward the main street. "If someone should see us coupling like this in broad daylight . . . ummm, faster! Harder!"

Ki obliged the mayor's daughter. He felt her shivering with ecstasy as her hips thrust harder and harder until she was biting his shoulder and trying to drown her cries of pleasure.

Ki battered her against the wall until his own body stiffened. He bared his teeth and growled like a tiger as he filled her with his seed.

She clung to him, panting and gasping for several minutes until the samurai at last lowered her to the ground. He had left her weak in the knees and unsteady but that would pass.

"I never had anyone like you before," she whispered. "Who *are* you?"

"A samurai."

"What. . . ."

Ki covered her lips with his forefinger. "It doesn't matter."

"Will I see you again?"

"Probably not."

She threw her arms around his neck and kissed him passionately. "I'll never forget you, samurai."

"Yes, you will," he said with a smile. "And if that young man tries to bother you again, tell him that you'll send for me and I'll kill him next time. That ought to do the trick."

"Where? Where can I send for you!"

But Ki didn't answer. Instead, he laughed, tucked his wet manhood into his trousers and headed back toward the main street. He felt much better now, refreshed, clear-minded and physically satisfied.

★

Chapter 22

Hastings Long paced up and down in his mining cabin while three of his favored men watched with growing anxiety.

"Something is very, very wrong," Long repeated over and over. "I should have heard from them by now. Should have had a telegram waiting for us in Carson City."

"Maybe Ki double-crossed us, Boss Man," a hatchet-faced man with a drooping mustache growled. "Shorty said he was gonna."

"Otis, I've taken that possibility into consideration," Long said. "And I think you are right. Either that, or they did find that buried gold and they split it up among themselves and lit out for parts unknown."

The men exchanged doubtful glances. One said, "So what are we going to do about it?"

"I need to go down there and find out for myself. We'll shut the mine down and leave a few guards. Tell the men to get ready to ride."

"You want to ride a horse, or shall we prepare your fancy English buggy?"

"The buggy will be fine," Long snapped. "We can also use it to carry our food, extra water, and grain for the horses. Now go and leave me alone to think."

The three men did as they were ordered and when they were gone, Long knelt before a huge iron safe, spun the combination, and swung open the heavy door. He removed a wad of hundred-dollar bills and inserted them into his wallet and he also removed a felt bag. After closing the door and relocking the safe, he carried the bag over to a table and opened it to reveal a Swiss-made telescopic sight.

Long held the sight up to his eye and aimed it out the window. He made a slight adjustment and then he studied one of his guards up on the canyon walls. The telescopic sight was a remarkable piece of work. It was perfectly mated to the custom-made German rifle that rested in his gun case.

Long unlocked the case and carefully removed the rifle. It was a thing of beauty and it had cost him a thousand dollars two years earlier. Its stock was very dark and hand-carved of wood from the Black Forest.

He attached the stock to the rifle and hefted the weapon, admiring its perfect balance. "Yes," he said to himself out loud as he smiled, "manhunting, the perfect sport."

It was early afternoon by the time Hastings Long led a small but very competent cadre of professional gunfighters out of the canyon.

"No one comes in while we're gone!" he called up to the four guards he had chosen to remain behind. "Is that clearly understood?"

They nodded. Long knew the guards would enter his cabin and attempt to open his safe. They'd fail, of course. But he'd see the evidence and he'd punish them later.

"What if we don't find them in Bullfrog?" a man named Otis Hays asked.

"Then we track them down and take retribution for their disloyalty."

Otis nodded. "And the girl?"

"She's mine," Long said. "If she's still alive."

Jessie and Ki were traveling light and fast on their return from Bullfrog. On their second night, they camped in a

153

jumble of rocks where the samurai had found a small spring for themselves and the horses.

"Two more days," Jessie said, looking northward through the rocks that shielded their small campfire from view. "I'm wondering how many men Hastings Long will have remaining with him now that we've wiped out those in Bullfrog."

"I don't know," the samurai told her. "But I would imagine he's got half a dozen or more left. I just had the feeling that he's got a pretty big operation."

"Then maybe we should go to Carson City first and enlist Sheriff Malloy's help. He could probably rouse a posse."

"It's your decision," the samurai said, not sounding very enthused about the idea. "But you know how things can get complicated when you get too many people involved."

"I know," Jessie said. "But we were pretty fortunate in Bullfrog. I'm not sure we can count on being as lucky a second time."

"We will be cunning," the samurai said. "I will go among them at night as *ninja*. In the morning, you will be able to walk into their canyon and only their leader will still be alive."

"All right," Jessie said with a half-smile. "We'll play it your way."

That night, a hard wind began to blow, and once when Jessie awoke she saw dark storm clouds sweeping along before the moon. At dawn a cold rain began to fall, but they stayed warm and dry by scooting under the rocks. The samurai had even collected enough brush and wood the night before and put it under cover so that they had a hot breakfast.

But by seven o'clock Jessie was tired of waiting for the storm to pass. "It could last for days," she reasoned as she pulled on the slicker she always carried tied behind her saddle. "I say we might as well push on. Maybe we can ride out from under the storm."

Ki was in full agreement and they were saddled and preparing to ride out within half an hour when Jessie said, "Look!"

154

The samurai turned to the north and followed Jessie's pointing finger. The corners of his mouth drew downward. "What do you make of them?"

Jessie shook her head. "I don't know. Six or seven riders and a buggy? You tell me."

"It could be him," Ki said, not needing to tell her who the "him" referred to.

"Yes, it could," Jessie agreed. "But it could also be someone important who believes in being well protected during his travels."

"So how do we find out?" Ki asked. "If it's Hastings Long, he'll recognize me in an instant."

Jessie dropped back down behind the rocks to think out loud. "If it's him, it would be too risky to show yourself. He's got too many men with him to fight and there's liable to be a few of them riding very fast horses. I don't think we can count on outrunning them if things went against us."

"But we can't just like them pass on by," the samurai said, his voice carrying a hint of protest. "And if you went out to see them, it would look pretty suspicious, a woman alone."

Jessie frowned. "How far back was the last mining town we rode through?"

"Twenty miles."

It was a difficult decision. Jessie hated the idea of following this group that far only to discover that they were not the remainder of the Black Bandana Gang.

She eased up and watched the buggy and the riders who were moving at a pretty good clip. They would pass about two miles to the east of where she and Ki were camped.

"They're in a hurry about something," she said. "I think we had better find out just what it is."

When the buggy and the riders passed, Ki and Jessie waited a half hour, then fell in behind them.

"What are we going to do if they don't stop at Gold Point?" Ki asked.

"Was that the name of that last mining settlement?"

"Yes."

Just as Jessie was about to speak, a huge bolt of lightning shivered out of the dark skies and it was followed a few seconds later by a roll of thunder. It began to rain much harder. So hard, in fact, that Jessie knew that the tracks she and Ki intended to follow might very well wash away before she could find them.

"I think they'll have to stop given this storm!" Jessie called as she tightened her cinch and mounted the dapple-gray mare.

"And I don't think we have to worry about losing them. They'll be heading for Gold Point just as fast as they can before that buggy gets mired down in the mud."

Ki mounted quickly and followed her out of the rocks. Hatless and foregoing a slicker, the rain pelted his face and he was quickly soaked to the skin.

Jessie spurred her mare south feeling the cold bite of the wind and rain. She hoped that it really was Hastings Long in that buggy because she wanted a showdown. If this was the last of the Black Bandana Gang who had caused so much death and misery, Jessie figured she'd let Ki whittle down the odds, *ninja* style, before she confronted the outlaw leader.

But remembering old Judge Milton Archibald, she knew she wanted Hastings Long in her own sights before this stormy day was through.

★

Chapter 23

Gold Point was not as prosperous as Bullfrog, but it had four saloons, a bank, two hotels, a general store, a weekly newspaper, and a brothel that could brag of a having a very hairy woman with buckteeth as its main attraction. The prostitute's working name was Little Ida Sue and it was said she charged a dollar more than any of the other girls and was well worth it.

When Hastings Long and his bedraggled gang rode into town, they tied their horses up before the nearest hotel and went straight inside.

"I need one room for myself, three or four for my men," Long said, dropping a twenty dollar bill on the hotel's registration desk.

"Gonna be here more than a week, I can give you the weekly rate," the old clerk offered.

"We're leaving first thing in the morning," Long growled, "unless it's snowing. Does it snow down this far south?"

"Not much. Leastways when it does, it melts right away."

"Good. Give me my change and the keys."

Long and his men wasted no time getting settled and a short time later, he called a meeting in his room. "You boys have been caged up at my mining operation for a good long while and since we can't go on, there's no reason why you shouldn't sow a few wild oats in this one-horse town."

The outlaws grinned. "Women and whiskey?"

"Yeah," Long said, peeling off twenties and handing a pair of them to each of his men. "But just don't get into any trouble. I want no killings tonight and nobody better get loose-lipped about who we are and just what we're going to do when we reach Bullfrog. Is that understood?"

The men nodded.

"All right then," Long said, "go let off some steam but I want want all of you back in your rooms by ten o'clock tonight."

"Can't you make that midnight, Boss Man?"

"No. And I'll be checking. We're after buried gold and until we find it, we are strictly up to business."

The outlaws nodded because they knew that Long did not tolerate any drunken rowdiness among his men.

When his men were all gone, Long went back downstairs and beckoned the hotel clerk to his side. He pulled out his money and peeled off a twenty. "I want a hot bath followed by a young, good-looking woman. Can you take care of that, old timer?"

"You bet I can."

"*Clean* water, *clean* woman. You understand me," Long said, his voice hardening.

"Yes sir!"

"All right. Get moving."

Long went up to his room and it was not ten minutes later that a knock sounded on his door.

"Who is it?" he called.

"Your bath."

Long opened the door with one hand while he held a gun in the other. When he was sure that everything was as promised, he stepped aside and watched as two young men carried in steaming buckets of water followed by a tin tub and a hard-faced woman with black hair and bright red lipstick.

"Your woman," she said.

158

"I said I wanted a clean, young woman," Long growled. "You don't look either."

The woman surprised him by smiling. "I'm as young as you are and as for being clean, have you looked at yourself in the mirror?"

Long glanced down at this suit which was mud-splattered. His buggy horse had thrown a lot of slop at him the last few miles into Gold Point.

"Gold Point isn't the Barbary Coast, mister," she said, "so maybe you shouldn't be so fussy. And maybe we could both use a bath and some of that fancy brandy you got sitting on your bedside table."

Long found himself admiring the floozy's brass. "Take your coat off and let's see what you've got to offer."

To his surprise, she was wearing nothing but skin under the long, heavy coat. And he was also surprised to see that she was a whole lot more appealing from the neck down. She had good, long legs and high, firm breasts. Her belly protruded a little and there was a wicked scar across her right thigh, but otherwise, she was just fine.

"Here," he said, uncorking the bottle and offering it to her. "It's imported French brandy. Costs fifty dollars a bottle."

"I cost fifty dollars a pop," she told him, arching her back and pushing her breasts out at him almost in a gesture of defiance.

"Fifty dollars?" Long barked a cold laugh. "Woman, you haven't been worth fifty dollars since you were a virgin and that's been at least twenty years ago."

To his amazement, she reached for her coat.

"Hey, what are you doing?"

"I'm leaving. Get drunk and play with yourself. I don't care."

"Are you crazy!"

She stopped buttoning the coat. "I don't like being insulted by rich sonsofbitches like you. I'd rather find a poor cowboy or miner who tells me I'm pretty and I screw like a well-oiled machine."

159

She was really leaving. "All right!" he snapped. "Fifty dollars. But for that kind of money, I damn sure don't feel that I got to compliment you."

The woman's hand froze at her button for a moment and then she pulled it free. She shrugged her shoulders and the coat fell to the floor. Somehow Long found the gesture incredibly provocative and he felt his manhood began to stiffen.

"So, you're not so proud after all," he said. "Just like all the rest of us, you have your price."

"That's right," she said. "For fifty dollars, good liquor, and a hot bath, you can even call me names while you're doing it to me."

He began to unbutton his pants and when he dropped them to the floor, his manhood popped out to stand at attention.

The woman's mouth formed a loose grin. "I thought you didn't want a dirty whore. I thought you wanted me to take that nice, hot bath first."

"The hell with that," Long panted, kicking off his boots and reaching for the woman. "We can get clean and drunk later."

Just before he slammed his rod into the woman, she said, "Rich or poor, once a man gets it up, they all come down to the same level."

Hastings Long supposed she was right. He didn't know her name and he didn't want to know her background. She was hard and cynical and she stunk and was dirty. None of that mattered when she moaned and her nice, professional body began to move against his just as smooth and hard as that of a snake.

Later, when they were finished and he reached for the bottle, she rolled over and laughed at him.

"What's so funny!" he demanded.

"You," she said. "You say you want me clean, but you don't. You want it all stinky and dirty."

"What are you, some kind of head doctor or do you just have a crystal ball up your ass?"

160

She began to laugh again. Only this time, it sounded better. "What the hell are you, anyway? A banker or a politician? Bet you got plenty of money."

"Who I am is none of your business. Your business is to pleasure me for the next few hours."

The laughter died on her lips. "Yeah," she said. "Fifty dollars is a lot of money. Probably as much as you've ever paid."

"I've paid more. A lot more," he said.

"Then you were wasting your money," she told him, throwing her long, pretty leg over his hip and taking hold of his tool and doing things to it that made his heart begin to thump harder.

"What's your name?"

"Does it matter?"

"No."

"Then don't ask. Or call me whatever you want. Some men call me Lucy. Some call me the name of their lost childhood sweetheart. Some have even called me 'mama.' "

"I'll call you whore." He challenged her with his eyes, wanting to see hurt but finding nothing.

"Well," he snapped, "what do you say about that, Whore?"

In reply, she grabbed his scrotum and squeezed it sharply. He gasped with pain and grabbed her by the throat. "I could break your neck for doing that!"

"Before you did," she choked, "I'd crush your grapes and then we'd both be up a shit creek without a paddle, wouldn't we?"

Long stared into her eyes and, for some crazy reason he could not explain, he kissed her hard on the mouth. She kissed him back and he felt an incredible rush of desire. So great that he made love to her again, not believing it was possible at his age.

Later, he poured the brandy down his gullet and let it burn because she seemed to look right through him. He wanted to tell her to go away, but couldn't. Crazy, wasn't it? With nice women or the most hardened men, he was the master.

161

But when it came to a low-down brassy whore, one like this who had guts and savvy, Hastings Long believed that he had met his match.

"I'm going to call you . . . Anna."

"Why?"

"I once had a puppy named Anna. I think it was the only thing I ever really loved."

She sat up quickly and reached for her coat.

"What the hell are you doing now!"

"I'm getting out of here."

He jumped off the bed and tore the coat from her hands. He grabbed her by the shoulders. "I don't want you to go."

"You had me twice. Keep your expensive French brandy and let me out of here."

"No," he said, "you're staying. And you're coming with me tomorrow. You'll sit beside me in my buggy."

"The hell I will!"

He shook her hard and she tried to claw his face, but he crushed her to his chest. "What the goddamn hell is the matter with you!"

"Don't call me Anna!"

He shook his head. "I'll call you something else. I'll call you Lucy. You said you'd been called that before."

"Did you ever know a Lucy?"

"No."

He felt her relax.

"All right," she told him. "For you, I'm Lucy."

"Get in the bath with me."

She snorted. "If we both get in there at the same time, half the water will pour out. Besides that, you know what we'll start doing again."

"Yeah," he said. "I know. Let's get in anyway. I can send for more water."

She got into the tub. It felt wonderful and she smiled. "Come on."

He climbed in facing her. It was a big tub but, even so, their feet were both sticking out of the water.

"Will you come with me tomorrow, Lucy?"

"What for?"

"I can't tell you that."

She studied his face. "I don't think I want to know anyway. And yeah, I'll come."

Long had not realized he'd been holding his breath for her reply. "Good," he said. "Good!"

She really smiled and then she dipped her head into the tub and threw it back, her black hair whipping water across the room. For just that instant, she looked almost like . . . like a schoolgirl he'd once known that he'd talked into going skinny-dipping in a pond and before he'd robbed her of her virginity and innocence. It had been one of the few things he'd done that he'd always regretted because the girl had changed, and much for the worse.

"What's the matter?" she asked suddenly.

"It's nothing, Lucy," he said, reaching way back for the bottle of brandy. "Nothing at all."

★

Chapter 24

Jessie had waited patiently for her samurai to return. Now, as he rejoined her, she said, "What did you find out?"

"They're all in the saloon drinking," Ki said. "They might go to another saloon or a brothel, but we'll have no trouble finding them."

"Let's go after Hastings Long," Jessie said. "Once we have him, the others will either give up or try and run away."

Ki and Jessie cut across the street to enter the hotel. There was an old man behind the registration desk.

"I'm afraid that I'm full up tonight," he said.

"We're looking for a man." Quickly, Jessie described Hastings Long, adding, "We saw him come in here a while ago and would like to pay him a little visit."

"Are you . . . friends of his?"

"Something like that," Jessie hedged.

"Well he's taking a bath right now. Maybe you ought to come back later."

"It won't wait," Jessie insisted.

But the old man was stubborn. "Yeah, but, well, I think he might have a visitor right now. Why don't you come back? Or . . . or leave a message. Yeah, do that and I'll slip it under his door."

Jessie glanced at Ki and the samurai took a menacing step forward. "The room number," he said. "Now!"

The hotel clerk looked into the samurai's eyes and whispered, "Room 107. Fourth door on your right down the hall."

"Thank you."

Ki and Jessie tiptoed down the carpeted hallway and when Jessie had her gun out and trained on the door, she nodded.

The samurai uncoiled into the air with tremendous power and his feet smashed into the door, knocking it completely off its hinges. Wood splintered and Ki landed on the falling door as Jessie came flying in behind.

"Freeze, both of you!" she shouted.

"Who the hell are you!" a black-haired woman sitting astraddle Hastings Long in the bathtub demanded.

"Get out of the tub, get dressed and leave," Ki ordered.

The woman started to argue, then thought better of it and climbed off of Long in silence. Dripping wet, she grabbed up a long coat and pulled it on, then began to button it up to her chin.

"Don't you have a dress or anything?" Jessie asked.

"Honey, in my business, clothes don't mean a thing. So what are you going to do with my friend?"

"I'm not going to do anything with him," Jessie said. "He's a killer and we're just taking him back to stand trial in Carson City. He's responsible for the deaths of a lot of good people up in that country."

"Don't you believe her, Lucy! I'm innocent!"

The woman hesitated and Jessie was forced to say, "I think you'd better go."

"They're going to *murder* me!" Long shouted. "Lucy, you got to help me!"

Lucy found a pair of high-heeled shoes and worked them onto her wet feet. She took a pull on the brandy bottle. "I'm sorry we won't be taking that drive tomorrow morning."

"They're after my money," Long whined, shaking his head back and forth. "If you won't help me, at least send for my boys. They're out there and they'll come help me."

"Listen," Jessie said, seeing the indecision and growing distress in the prostitute's dark eyes, "his 'boys' are all killers and thieves. They're members of the Black Bandana Gang. Just stay out of this. Please!"

Jessie thought the woman was listening to her and on her way out of the door but, suddenly, Lucy whirled and drew a derringer from her coat pocket and shoved it into Jessie's ribs.

"Now *you* drop the gun."

Jessie's shoulders slumped with defeat. "You don't know what you're doing!"

"Drop it or I'll shoot! And tell your friend if he so much as blinks I'll kill you."

Jessie dropped her gun and Long hopped out of the tub laughing. "Lucy," he cried, "you're the best find I've ever made. You and me are going far together, honey!"

Long carefully dried himself with a towel before he found a sixgun under his pillow and cocked back the hammer.

"Lucy, you're my witness. This pair tried to rob and kill us," he said, thinking out loud. "Yeah, that's it. They kicked down my door and tried to rob and kill us."

The woman said nothing. Long pointed his sixgun at Ki. "You first because you tricked me."

"That's right," Ki said, trying to bid for some time, "and it was easy."

Long's cheeks flushed. "I only regret I haven't time to see you die slow and in agony."

Jessie gathered herself to jump at the man.

"No!" the whore protested loudly. "You can't just murder them."

"Hell," Long argued, "you'd have shot her if she hadn't dropped her gun."

"I said I would," the woman stammered, "but I was bluffing."

"Well, Lucy, I damn sure ain't. Adios, Ki!"

Lucy raised her derringer and pointed it at Hastings Long. "No," she said, her voice threatening to crack. "I won't let you execute them. Let them go!"

Long shook his head. "Can't do that, honey. Now, if you can't stand the sight of their blood, then git!"

"Drop your gun."

Long's eyebrows raised in a question. "You'd shoot *me*?"

"I hardly know you. And maybe, maybe I don't know you at all."

Long thought about that for a moment and then he turned his gun on Lucy. "I ain't bluffing, honey. Drop that gun and get out of here. In the morning, we'll head north together in my fancy carriage that'll make you feel like a queen. I'll show you the Comstock Lode in the grandest style you ever did see. Buy you champagne by the keg and a dress made of silver dollars."

But the woman shook her head. "I couldn't live knowing you murdered these two. I'm not much, but I draw the line at executions."

Long clucked his tongue. "And just when I thought you and I were going to make a real pair. Lucy, honey, you don't know how disappointed I am and how much I hate to do this."

The gun in Long's fist belched fire and smoke as Jessie threw herself at the woman knowing it was too late. They crashed to the floor and Jessie scooped up the derringer and twisted in time to see the samurai attack.

Long's gun fired once more but the samurai ducked under the weapon and the heel of his right hand swept upward into Long's nose. Jessie heard a sickening crunch of splintering bone as Long screamed, the bones of his nose driving up into his brain.

Jessie turned back to the woman. There was a neat bullet hole in her forehead.

"Are you all right?" Ki asked.

"Yes," Jessie replied, climbing a little unsteadily to her feet.

"Why don't you stay here with her and I'll go finish this," the samurai suggested in a gentle voice as he removed a star blade from his tunic.

But Jessie shook her head. "We're seeing this thing through all the way together."

Without needing words, they headed back down the hall and across the lobby.

"Hey!" the hotel clerk cried. "What'd you do, kill 'em!"

Jessie and Ki didn't answer. People were flocking toward the hotel and Jessie hoped that what remained of the Black Bandana Gang had been preoccupied enough that they either hadn't heard the shots or weren't curious enough to leave their entertainment.

When they entered the saloon, the outlaws were still together, drinking and joking.

"Party is over," Jessie said, gun lifting in her fist. "Hands up!"

There were four of them and the stupidest went for his sidearm. Jessie fired from the hip and the man died with a look of confusion flooding across his glazing eyes.

"Anyone else?" Ki asked softly, the *shuriken* star blade plainly visible.

They shook their heads.

"Bartender," Jessie called.

A head poked over the top of the bar. "Miss?"

"Find us a length of rope or even some baling wire and then tie these men's wrists behind their backs. They're outlaws wanted for murder in Reno, Virginia City, and Carson City."

"Yes, ma'am!"

A big crowd formed outside the saloon but no one dared to come inside. When the outlaws were tied up, Jessie said, "Let's get them on their horses and get out of here."

"What about her?" Ki asked.

Jessie knew full well that "her" was the woman who had just saved their lives in the hotel room.

She turned to the bartender, but she was speaking to everyone in the room. "There's a dead woman in the hotel down the street. Black hair. Early forties. Bad scar right here."

168

Jessie pointed to her own right thigh. "Anyone know her name?"

"Sure," the bartender said, "don't know her last name 'cause she never told it to anyone. But a few of us knew her real first name was Anna."

"Anna," Jessie repeated. She reached into her pants and dragged out a wad of bills, then walked over and dropped them on the bar.

"I want everyone in the room to toast Anna and then I want fifty dollars of that money to buy her the best funeral Gold Point has ever seen. I want the best casket and her lying in it wearing the finest dress that can be found in this town. Is that understood?"

The bartender nodded. "Anna had a lot of friends in Gold Point. Don't worry, we won't do wrong by her."

A number of men nodded in agreement and several looked like they might even be upset enough to shed tears.

Satisfied, she turned and followed Ki and their prisoners out to their horses.

When they were mounted and ready to leave, Ki said, "There are bound to be a few of this gang left to guard Long's mining operation up in that box canyon we've got a map for. I can take them alive—or dead."

Jessie climbed wearily on her horse. "Let's let Sheriff Malloy and a few of his friends do that. He needs to win some votes for the next election."

"Whatever you say."

"Let's ride!" Jessie ordered, reining her horse north and thinking that Anna was one of her favorite names.

Watch for

LONE STAR IN THE TIMBERLANDS

118th novel in the exciting LONE STAR series
from Jove

Coming in June!

It was late afternoon when I got on my horse and rode the half mile from the house I'd built for Nora, my wife, up to the big ranch house my father and my two younger brothers still occupied. I had good news, the kind of news that does a body good, and I had taken the short run pretty fast. The two-year-old bay colt I'd been riding lately was kind of surprised when I hit him with the spurs, but he'd been lazing around the little horse trap behind my house and was grateful for the chance to stretch his legs and impress me with his speed. So we made it over the rolling plains of our ranch, the Half-Moon, in mighty good time.

I pulled up just at the front door of the big house, dropped the reins to the ground so that the colt would stand, and then made my way up on the big wooden porch, the rowels of my spurs making a *ching-ching* sound as I walked. I opened the big front door and let myself into the hall that led back to the main parts of the house.

I was Justa Williams and I was boss of all thirty-thousand deeded acres of the place. I had been so since it had become my duty on the weakening of our father, Howard, through two unfortunate incidents. The first had been the early demise of our mother, which had taken it out of Howard. That had been when he'd sort of started preparing me to take over the load. I'd been a hard sixteen or a soft seventeen at the time. The next level had jumped up when he'd got nicked in the lungs by a stray bullet. After that I'd had the job of boss. The place was run with my two younger brothers, Ben and Norris.

It had been a hard job but having Howard around had made the job easier. Now I had some good news for him and I meant him to take it so. So when I went clumping back toward his bedroom that was just off the office I went to yelling, "Howard! Howard!"

He'd been lying back on his daybed, and he got up at my approach and come out leaning on his cane. He said, "What the thunder!"

I said, "Old man, sit down."

I went over and poured us out a good three fingers of whiskey. I didn't ever bother to water his as I was supposed to do because my news was so big. He looked on with a good deal of pleasure as I poured out the drink. He wasn't even supposed to drink whiskey, but he'd put up such a fuss that the doctor had finally given in and allowed him one well-watered whiskey a day. But Howard claimed he never could count very well and that sometimes he got mixed up and that one drink turned into four. But, hell, I couldn't blame him. Sitting around all day like he was forced to was enough to make anybody crave a drink even if it was just for something to do.

But now he seen he was going to get the straight stuff and he got a mighty big gleam in his eye. He took the glass when I handed it to him and said, "What's the occasion? Tryin' to kill me off?"

"Hell no," I said. "But a man can't make a proper toast with watered whiskey."

"That's a fact," he said. "Now what the thunder are we toasting?"

I clinked my glass with his. I said, "If all goes well you are going to be a grandfather."

"Lord A'mighty!" he said.

We said, "Luck" as was our custom and then knocked them back.

176

Then he set his glass down and said, "Well, I'll just be damned." He got a satisfied look on his face that I didn't reckon was all due to the whiskey. He said, "Been long enough in coming."

I said, "Hell, the way you keep me busy with this ranch's business I'm surprised I've had the time."

"Pshaw!" he said.

We stood there, kind of enjoying the moment, and then I nodded at the whiskey bottle and said, "You keep on sneaking drinks, you ain't likely to be around for the occasion."

He reared up and said, "Here now! When did I raise you to talk like that?"

I gave him a small smile and said, "Somewhere along the line." Then I set my glass down and said, "Howard, I've got to get to work. I just reckoned you'd want the news."

He said, "Guess it will be a boy?"

I give him a sarcastic look. I said, "Sure, Howard, and I've gone into the gypsy business."

Then I turned out of the house and went to looking for our foreman, Harley. It was early spring in the year of 1898, and we were coming into a swift calf crop after an unusually mild winter. We were about to have calves dropping all over the place, and with the quality of our crossbred beef, we couldn't afford to lose a one.

On the way across the ranch yard my youngest brother, Ben, came riding up. He was on a little prancing chestnut that wouldn't stay still while he was trying to talk to me. I knew he was schooling the little filly, but I said, a little impatiently, "Ben, either ride on off and talk to me later or make that damn horse stand. I can't catch but every other word."

Ben said, mildly, "Hell, don't get agitated. I just wanted to give you a piece of news you might be interested in."

I said, "All right, what is this piece of news?"

"One of the hands drifting the Shorthorn herd got sent back to the barn to pick up some stuff for Harley. He said he seen Lew Vara heading this way."

I was standing up near his horse. The animal had been worked pretty hard, and you could take the horse smell right up your nose off him. I said, "Well, okay. So the sheriff is coming. What you reckon we ought to do, get him a cake baked?"

He give me one of his sardonic looks. Ben and I were so much alike it was awful to contemplate. Only difference between us was that I was a good deal wiser and less hot-headed, and he was an even size smaller than me. He said, "I reckon he'd rather have whiskey."

I said, "I got some news for you but I ain't going to tell you now."

"What is it?"

I wasn't about to tell him he might be an uncle under such circumstances. I gave his horse a whack on the rump and said, as he went off, "Tell you this evening after work. Now get, and tell Ray Hays I want to see him later on."

He rode off, and I walked back to the ranch house thinking about Lew Vara. Lew, outside of my family, was about the best friend I'd ever had. We'd started off, however, in a kind of peculiar way to make friends. Some eight or nine years past Lew and I had had about the worst fistfight I'd ever been in. It occurred at Crook's Saloon and Cafe in Blessing, the closest town to our ranch, about seven miles away, of which we owned a good part. The fight took nearly a half an hour and we both did our dead level best to beat the other to death. I won the fight, but unfairly. Lew had had me down on the saloon floor and was in the process of finishing me off when my groping hand found a beer mug. I smashed him over the head with it in a last-ditch effort to keep my own head on my shoulders. It sent Lew to the infirmary for quite a long stay; I'd fractured his skull. When he was partially recovered Lew sent word to me that as soon as he was able, he was coming to kill me.

But it never happened. When he was free from medical care Lew took off for the Oklahoma Territory, and I didn't hear another word from him for four years. Next time I saw him he came into that very same saloon. I was sitting at a

178

back table when I saw him come through the door. I eased my right leg forward so as to clear my revolver for a quick draw from the holster. But Lew just came up, stuck out his hand in a friendly gesture, and said he wanted to let bygones be bygones. He offered to buy me a drink, but I had a bottle on the table so I just told him to get himself a glass and take advantage of my hospitality.

Which he did.

After that Lew became a friend of the family and was important in helping the Williams family in about three confrontations where his gun and his savvy did a good deal to turn the tide in our favor. After that we ran him against the incumbent sheriff who we'd come to dislike and no longer trust. Lew had been reluctant at first, but I'd told him that money couldn't buy poverty but it could damn well buy the sheriff's job in Matagorda County. As a result he got elected, and so far as I was concerned, he did an outstanding job of keeping the peace in his territory.

Which wasn't saying a great deal because most of the trouble he had to deal with, outside of helping us, was the occasional Saturday night drunk and the odd Main Street dogfight.

So I walked back to the main ranch house wondering what he wanted. But I also knew that if it was in my power to give, Lew could have it.

I was standing on the porch about five minutes later when he came riding up. I said, "You want to come inside or talk outside?"

He swung off his horse. He said, "Let's get inside."

"You want coffee?"

"I could stand it."

"This going to be serious?"

"Is to me."

"All right."

I led him through the house to the dining room, where we generally, as a family, sat around and talked things out. I said, looking at Lew, "Get started on it."

179

He wouldn't face me. "Wait until the coffee comes. We can talk then."

About then Buttercup came staggering in with a couple of cups of coffee. It didn't much make any difference about what time of day or night it was, Buttercup might or might not be staggering. He was an old hand of our father's who'd helped to develop the Half-Moon. In his day he'd been about the best horse breaker around, but time and tumbles had taken their toll. But Howard wasn't a man to forget past loyalties so he'd kept Buttercup on as a cook. His real name was Butterfield, but me and my brothers had called him Buttercup, a name he clearly despised, for as long as I could remember. He was easily the best shot with a long-range rifle I'd ever seen. He had an old .50-caliber Sharps buffalo rifle, and even with his old eyes and seemingly unsteady hands he was deadly anywhere up to five hundred yards. On more than one occasion I'd had the benefit of that seemingly ageless ability. Now he set the coffee down for us and gave all the indications of making himself at home. I said, "Buttercup, go on back out in the kitchen. This is a private conversation."

I sat. I picked up my coffee cup and blew on it and then took a sip. I said, "Let me have it, Lew."

He looked plain miserable. He said, "Justa, you and your family have done me a world of good. So has the town and the county. I used to be the trash of the alley and y'all helped bring me back from nothing." He looked away. He said, "That's why this is so damn hard."

"What's so damned hard?"

But instead of answering straight out he said, "They is going to be people that don't understand. That's why I want you to have the straight of it."

I said, with a little heat, "Goddammit, Lew, if you don't tell me what's going on I'm going to stretch you out over that kitchen stove in yonder."

He'd been looking away, but now he brought his gaze back to me and said, "I've got to resign, Justa. As sheriff. And not only that, I got to quit this part of the country."

Thoughts of his past life in the Oklahoma Territory flashed through my mind, when he'd been thought an outlaw and later proved innocent. I thought maybe that old business had come up again and he was going to have to flee for his life and his freedom. I said as much.

He give me a look and then made a short bark that I reckoned he took for a laugh. He said, "Naw, you got it about as backwards as can be. It's got to do with my days in the Oklahoma Territory all right, but it ain't the law. Pretty much the opposite of it. It's the outlaw part that's coming to plague me."

It took some doing, but I finally got the whole story out of him. It seemed that the old gang he'd fallen in with in Oklahoma had got wind of his being the sheriff of Matagorda County. They thought that Lew was still the same young hellion and that they had them a bird nest on the ground, what with him being sheriff and all. They'd sent word that they'd be in town in a few days and they figured to "pick the place clean." And they expected Lew's help.

"How'd you get word?"

Lew said, "Right now they are raising hell in Galveston, but they sent the first robin of spring down to let me know to get the welcome mat rolled out. Some kid about eighteen or nineteen. Thinks he's tough."

"Where's he?"

Lew jerked his head in the general direction of Blessing. "I throwed him in jail."

I said, "You got me confused. How is you quitting going to help the situation? Looks like with no law it would be even worse."

He said, "If I ain't here maybe they won't come. I plan to send the robin back with the message I ain't the sheriff and ain't even in the country. Besides, there's plenty of good men in the county for the job that won't attract the riffraff I seem to have done." He looked down at his coffee as if he was ashamed.

I didn't know what to say for a minute. This didn't sound like the Lew Vara I knew. I understood he wasn't afraid

181

and I understood he thought he was doing what he thought was the best for everyone concerned, but I didn't think he was thinking too straight. I said, "Lew, how many of them is there?"

He said, tiredly, "About eighteen all told. Counting the robin in the jail. But they be a bunch of rough hombres. This town ain't equipped to handle such. Not without a whole lot of folks gettin' hurt. And I won't have that. I figured on an argument from you, Justa, but I ain't going to make no battlefield out of this town. I know this bunch. Or kinds like them." Then he raised his head and give me a hard look. "So I don't want no argument out of you. I come out to tell you what was what because I care about what you might think of me. Don't make me no mind about nobody else but I wanted you to know."

I got up. I said, "Finish your coffee. I got to ride over to my house. I'll be back inside of half an hour. Then we'll go into town and look into this matter."

He said, "Dammit, Justa, I done told you I—"

"Yeah, I know what you told me. I also know it ain't really what you want to do. Now we ain't going to argue and I ain't going to try to tell you what to do, but I am going to ask you to let us look into the situation a little before you light a shuck and go tearing out of here. Now will you wait until I ride over to the house and tell Nora I'm going into town?"

He looked uncomfortable, but, after a moment, he nodded. "All right," he said. "But it ain't going to change my mind none."

I said, "Just go in and visit with Howard until I get back. He don't get much company and even as sorry as you are you're better than nothing."

That at least did make him smile a bit. He sipped at his coffee, and I took out the back door to where my horse was waiting.

Nora met me at the front door when I came into the house. She said, "Well, how did the soon-to-be grandpa take it?"

182

I said, "Howard? Like to have knocked the heels off his boots. I give him a straight shot of whiskey in celebration. He's so damned tickled I don't reckon he's settled down yet."

"What about the others?"

I said, kind of cautiously, "Well, wasn't nobody else around. Ben's out with the herd and Norris is in Blessing. Naturally Buttercup was drunk."

Meanwhile I was kind of edging my way back toward our bedroom. She followed me. I was at the point of strapping on my gunbelt when she came into the room. She said, "Why are you putting on that gun?"

It was my sidegun, a 42/40-caliber Colts revolver that I'd been carrying for several years. I had two of them, one that I wore and one that I carried in my saddlebags. The gun was a .40-caliber chambered weapon on a .42-caliber frame. The heavier frame gave it a nice feel in the hand with very little barrel deflection, and the .40-caliber slug was big enough to stop any thing you could hit solid. It had been good luck for me and the best proof of that was that I was alive.

I said, kind of looking away from her, "Well, I've got to go into town."

"Why do you need your gun to go into town?"

I said, "Hell, Nora, I never go into town without a gun. You know that."

"What are you going into town for?"

I said, "Norris has got some papers for me to sign."

"I thought Norris was already in town. What does he need you to sign anything for?"

I kind of blew up. I said, "Dammit, Nora, what is with all these questions? I've got business. Ain't that good enough for you?"

She give me a cool look. "Yes," she said. "I don't mess in your business. It's only when you try and lie to me. Justa, you are the worst liar in the world."

"All right," I said. "All right. Lew Vara has got some trouble. Nothing serious. I'm going to give him a hand. God knows he's helped us out enough." I could hear her

183

maid, Juanita, banging around in the kitchen. I said, "Look, why don't you get Juanita to hitch up the buggy and you and her go up to the big house and fix us a supper. I'll be back before dark and we'll all eat together and celebrate. What about that?"

She looked at me for a long moment. I could see her thinking about all the possibilities. Finally she said, "Are you going to run a risk on the day I've told you you're going to be a father?"

"Hell no!" I said. "What do you think? I'm going in to use a little influence for Lew's sake. I ain't going to be running any risks."

She made a little motion with her hand. "Then why the gun?"

"Hell, Nora, I don't even ride out into the pasture without a gun. Will you quit plaguing me?"

It took a second, but then her smooth, young face calmed down. She said, "I'm sorry, honey. Go and help Lew if you can. Juanita and I will go up to the big house and I'll personally see to supper. You better be back."

I give her a good, loving kiss and then made my adieus, left the house, and mounted my horse and rode off.

But I rode off with a little guilt nagging at me. I swear, it is hell on a man to answer all the tugs he gets on his sleeve. He gets pulled first one way and then the other. A man damn near needs to be made out of India rubber to handle all of them. No, I wasn't riding into no danger that March day, but if we didn't do something about it, it wouldn't be long before I would be.

184

From the Creators of Longarm!

LONE☆STAR

Featuring the beautiful Jessica Starbuck
and her loyal half-American half-
Japanese martial arts sidekick Ki.